How To Use Your Decide Your Destiny Book

Follow the instructions below before reading this book.

1. Go to: www.doctorwhochildrensbooks.co.uk/decideyourdestiny

2. Click 'Begin' to launch the book selection screen.

3. After selecting your book, the scene selection menu will appear.

4. Start reading the story on page 1 of this book and follow the instructions at the end of each section.

5. When you make a decision that takes you online, select the correct box and enter the corresponding code word as prompted.

6. After watching the scene or completing your online activity, return to the scene selection screen and continue your story.

Now turn the page and begin your adventure!

The gas refinery is huge — two square miles of giant steel storage tanks, filters and chimneys. Industrial pipes surround the refinery like a gigantic nest of metallic snakes — some are no thicker than your arm; others are wide enough to stand upright inside. It all looks overwhelmingly complex.

Rising up from the centre of the refinery site is the Control Tower — a huge concrete cylinder topped by a ring of windows overlooking the entire development.

A long underground corridor leads from the car park to the reception area at the base of the Control Tower. It's busy here — full of people going about their business. Engineers, scientists, company executives, all on their way somewhere important.

Your school party is standing in front of the main reception desk, waiting for visitor passes to be issued. There are two teachers and about fifteen kids in your group. Everyone seems a little nervous — and no one is looking forward to the tour. A school trip to a gas refinery? No thanks!

But your attention has been caught by something on the far side of the reception area — a door marked NO UNAUTHORISED ACCESS. It's been left open.

No one seems to have noticed it except you.

But now your school party has been given their passes and are being led away for the tour of the factory. They're waving at you to come and join them. Someone's shouting out, full of excitement. They've found something interesting already. Perhaps the tour won't be so bad after all...

You glance back at the open door and read the sign again, wondering...

Really, you should stick with the tour party and see what they've found on 89.

But if you'd rather see what's on the other side of the door, go to 50.

'Quickly,' you say, 'let's block the pipe — we might be able to stop the gas coming in!'

You take off your jacket, screw it up into a ball and try stuffing it into the pipe.

'You won't get it past the grille,' the Doctor points out. 'Here — let me help!'

He sonics the grille and it falls away from the end of the pipe. Choking and gasping, you stuff the jacket right into the open end. The hissing is subdued.

The Doctor helps Amy to her feet. 'That's given us a little time,' he says. 'Good thinking!'

'Look,' Amy says, pointing. 'There's another exit!'

The Doctor's on it straight away, unlocking a door that lies flat to the metal wall opposite the entrance hatch. 'Let's see where it leads!'

You emerge in fresh air — thankfully — in what appears to be a modern, brightly-lit laboratory. A complicated network of pipes and tubes runs through the lab, some filled with bubbling liquids, others with slowly-moving gas vapour.

'Wait here,' the Doctor advises. He inspects the equipment quickly, scampering from workstation to workstation. 'This is interesting,' he murmurs, 'very interesting...'

'What have you found?' asks Amy.

'It's just as I thought,' replies the Doctor anxiously. He waves at the test tubes and gas filters. 'This gas is highly toxic – and serves a specific purpose. It gives life to a race of giant alien crabs called the Macra. If they're here, then it could mean trouble for all of us...'

He crosses to the far side of the lab and disappears through another connecting door.

You look at Amy. 'Where's he off to now?'

She shrugs. 'You never know with him. But what's that racket all about?'

If you listen carefully, you can hear a clanging noise – like something heavy being struck against metal walls. 'That doesn't sound too good.'

'We'd better catch up with the Doctor,' Amy says.

Catch up with him on 113.

'This way,' says the Doctor, turning his sonic screwdriver on the door. It slides open and he ushers you through. The door slides shut behind you.

But now you're all in a darkened passageway that smells distinctly of—

'Rotten eggs!' whispers Amy, horrified. 'Yeeeurrgh!'

'Hydrogen sulphide,' the Doctor nods, sniffing deeply. 'What's that doing in a gas refinery?'

'There must be all kinds of pongs in a gasworks,' you say.

'This company is in the business of turning natural gas into cheap energy,' replies the Doctor. 'Not stink bombs.'

He starts down the passageway, sniffing, following his nose like a bloodhound. Amy shrugs at you and follows.

You reach a junction in the passage. It looks like you're in some kind of gas pipe – one leads to the left, one to the right.

Which way should you go?

If you want to follow the right-hand passage, go to 110.

If you prefer to try the left-hand passage, go to 82.

Quickly, you follow the girl through the door.

And the man with the tweed jacket and hair is looking brightly at both the girl and you.

'How...' you begin, a little perplexed.

'Yeah, how d'you do?' the man says, waving rather than offering his hand. But then his attention switches to the girl. 'Who's your new friend, Amy?'

The girl turns to look at you, faintly bemused. 'No idea. Must have followed me in.'

'Er...' you begin again.

'Never mind,' declares the man. 'I'm the Doctor, this is Amy, you're going back to your school trip.'

He grasps you by the arm — he's surprisingly strong — and steers you back towards the door.

But it slams shut in his face. The Doctor huffs with annoyance, tries the door, finds it locked. 'As if I didn't have enough to do already,' he mutters despairingly, taking out a slim cylindrical device from his jacket pocket. 'Hang on. Sonic screwdriver. Have the door open in a jiffy.'

'Oh, hang on again!' He holds the screwdriver up. It's emitting a weird electric signal. 'Now that's odd. Don't you think that's odd?

I think it's odd.'

He walks around the room, holding the sonic screwdriver aloft, listening carefully to the strange warbling noise.

'Doctor,' says Amy. 'We're supposed to be checking the pipeline, remember!'

'Yes, pipeline, got it. But I'm picking up this rather strange signal... and it's so interesting!'

If you think the Doctor should check the pipeline, check out 115.

If you think he should investigate the strange signals, turn to 103.

You take the lift straight up. There's a tense few seconds until it slows and the doors hum open.

'No guards,' you realise, stepping out into an empty foyer.

'Yet,' says Amy.

The Doctor hurries across to the exit and checks to see what's outside. 'We're at the heart of the refinery,' he says softly. 'Nowhere near the reception area, the TARDIS, or your school party.'

'I don't mind,' you tell him. 'This is better than any school trip!'

'It won't last forever,' the Doctor warns you. 'We have to find a way to stop the Macra and close down the refinery. But first we need to get to the computer system that controls the gas flow. And to do that, we need to get past those guards.'

You peer out. There are two men in GasTech uniforms carrying sub-machine guns. They're standing with their backs to you.

Carefully, the three of you creep past the guards. One sound and they will be alerted.

The Doctor motions you across to a small access hatch set in the side of a huge silo. He unlocks the door and crawls inside. Silently, you follow with Amy.

It's dark and cold and damp and smells of Macra.

'Which way now?' you ask.

'Straight on, of course,' replies the Doctor, heading into the darkness.

Follow him to 128.

'On your feet, Professor!' says the Doctor, hauling the old man up.

The professor points groggily at a side door. 'That way, Doctor!'

You help the Doctor carry the scientist out through the door, with Amy following. The Macra roars inside the room, smashing the furniture to pieces. Its giant claws hammer dents in the metal walls as it tries to tear its way out.

'That was close,' you say.

'Follow the road down,' advises Professor Greif. 'It's an escape route I have kept ready for emergencies.'

You follow the rough path down, away from the refinery. The giant gas towers and silos stand tall against the clouds as you look back up. You wonder how many more Macra there are inside...

'The refinery was built close to the sea,' Professor Greif tells you weakly. 'It uses the seawater as a coolant, pumping it through underground pipes.'

The path leads down through a series of cliffs to the edge of a small inlet. There is a jetty with a speedboat moored at the end. You help Amy assist the professor into the boat while the Doctor uses his sonic screwdriver to start the outboard motor.

Sitting at the rear of the speedboat, the Doctor's face lights up with glee as he powers the craft away from the jetty and heads out of the tiny natural harbour.

The speedboat bounces over the waves – it's great to feel the wind and sea spray in your hair. But suddenly the professor lets out a deep groan and collapses to the floor of the boat.

If you think the professor is dying, go to 40.

If you think he's just seasick, go to 133.

'We need to get back to the Control Tower – quickly,' says the Doctor.

He seems to find his way through the labyrinthine factory very easily; it's a struggle to keep up with him.

Eventually he opens an access door at the base of the tower and bursts into the reception area.

Everyone inside, including your school party, turns to look.

'All right,' announces the Doctor loudly. 'No need to panic – but I really need you to move quickly to a place of safety. Things are about to get very, very dangerous here...'

There is a stunned silence, and nobody moves.

The Doctor sighs. 'OK, maybe you should just panic a little bit.'

Suddenly, the Doctor is leading everyone towards the exit doors. He opens them and waves everyone through.

'Wait a second!' cries Amy. 'Where have the schoolies all gone?'

'They've taken the other exit!' you realise. Instinctively, you go to help, but the Doctor grabs your arm.

'You stay with me,' he orders, in the kind of voice that you can't argue with. 'Amy, get after those kids. And watch out for you-know-what.'

'You-know-what?' you repeat, frowning.

The Doctor glowers. 'Just hope you don't have to find out.'

Go straight to 114.

The Doctor slams shut the door and you catch your breath for a moment.

Amy notices you looking at them both wide-eyed.

'We're here to find out what the Macra are up to,' she explains. 'They're aliens from another planet, and they shouldn't be here at all.'

The Doctor is sniffing the air like a bloodhound. 'Gas — they feed on certain gases that are poisonous to human beings. That's what they're here for. The question is — how? And what are we going to do about it?'

You might think that this would be a good time to rejoin your school party — but the Doctor is having none of it. 'No time for that. We need to follow that Macra! The sonic blast will have given it quite a headache — I was aiming straight down its gullet, towards the soft-tissue areas around the cerebral cortex. It'll be sick and confused, and probably head back to wherever it feels safest.'

'The lair of the Macra?' you suggest.

He smiles brightly. 'You catch on quick! Come on!'

He leads you both back into the vast metal chamber. There's no sign of the Macra now. But on the far side of the room are two doorways. One is much larger than the other, leading to a wide duct. Something as large as a Macra could go down that easily.

'And the other door?' wonders Amy.

The Doctor peeps through a narrow window in the top of the smaller door. 'Some kind of workshop,' he whispers. 'Looks promising — and smells promising too…'

If you want to check out the lab, go to 92.

If you want to follow the Macra, go to 30.

You step through the door and quickly try to take in your surroundings. The refinery is huge and complicated and it's hard to get your bearings. But before you can work out where you are — *Crack!* There's a blinding pain as something hard and heavy hits you from behind. Your senses spin and the world disappears in a dark, dizzying void.

If you want to see the Macra, click on box A on screen and enter the code word MACRA.

Or go straight to 97.

Stealthily, you approach the flames and the circle of Macra. The firelight illuminates the Doctor's face, which is a picture of fascination. Amy looks slightly more anxious.

'What are they doing?'

'Unless I'm very much mistaken,' whispers the Doctor, 'they're worshipping something. I never knew the Macra had a deity or belief system — other than ripping off other planets for gas and mineral rights.'

In the centre of the flames is a raised platform — a dais — and on top of the platform, surrounded by a ring of fire, is the statue of a Macra.

It appears to be carved from some kind of rust-coloured stone, a craggy and brutal effigy of a giant crab, its massive pincers at rest before it.

But then you notice something odd — the crusty eyestalks are moving slightly... and on the tips are two glossy black orbs reflecting the blaze!

Suddenly, the giant stone crab appears to move! It shuffles around on the dais as the other Macra clack their pincers in excitement.

'It's alive!' hisses the Doctor. 'Ancient and calcified — but alive! Must be one of the oldest Macra in existence!'

'Here on Earth?'

'Right here on Earth! How amazing is that?' The Doctor's voice is full of surprised delight. Then, his face falls. 'But we can't allow that. The Macra have no place on this planet.'

Quietly he circles around the outside of the worshipping Macra. Luckily their full concentration is on the ancient Macra on the altar.

'What are you looking for?' you ask, following the Doctor.

'The Macra can only survive down here by pumping their atmospheric gases into the cavern from the refinery,' he explains. 'Smell that air – you can detect the fumes quite easily. So there must be pipes leading down here somewhere. If we can find those...'

You spot them first – a series of pipes snaking down from the roof of the cavern. In the firelight you can see the valves on the end.

'We can cut off the flow of gas right here,' says the Doctor. 'All we have to do is turn the valves.'

'But which way?'

If you think you should turn the valves clockwise, go to 52.

If you think you should turn them anti-clockwise, go to 38.

The central column glows and the TARDIS dematerialises. The Doctor hurries around the controls, fine-tuning whatever mechanisms govern the flight of this remarkable space-time machine.

Eventually he throws a lever and the ship lands with a roar of its engines.

The Doctor then dashes out through the double doors, with Amy and you close on his heels.

The police box has landed in what looks like a cupboard. There's not much room — it's crammed into this gloomy space. You can see brooms and buckets and some janitor uniforms hanging on pegs.

'Well done, Doctor,' smiles Amy. 'You've found the cleaning cupboard!'

The exit is locked — but it's the work of a moment with the sonic screwdriver to open it. The three of you tumble out into some kind of darkened passageway.

'Ha!' cries the Doctor triumphantly. 'Not so far off after all!'

If you think the Doctor meant to come here, go to 92.

If you think you're in the wrong place, go to 100.

You race after the Doctor and Amy.

The Doctor is scanning the area with his sonic screwdriver, like a bloodhound searching out a trail.

'Thought I told you to stick with your chums on the factory tour,' he murmurs as you catch up. 'Or don't you ever do as you're told?'

'Sometimes,' you reply. 'At the moment I'd rather stick with you. I've got a feeling I'll learn more that way.'

He looks at you, his eyes glittering eagerly. 'You might find out more than you bargained for.'

'What are you doing here? What are you searching for?'

'The gas company's big secret!'

'What is it?'

'I don't know – it's a secret!'

The sonic screwdriver bleeps loudly and the Doctor jumps. 'This is it! Massive concentration of highly toxic gases – some of them in the praxis range, so we'd better be careful.'

'Praxis range?'

'Not a gas normally associated with this planet...'

What!?

But the Doctor's said enough. He stops dead and then suddenly turns to Amy. 'I've just had a nasty thought, Amy. You'd better round up the rest of our friend's school party. They're wandering around the refinery and right now it could be very dangerous!'

If you want to help Amy find your school party, go to 77.

If you'd rather stick with the Doctor, go to 114.

You push open the door. Beyond is a darkened corridor. There are cobwebs hanging from the ceiling and you can feel the grime underfoot. No one's been down here for years – probably not since the refinery was built.

You're about to turn back when you hear something.

You stop and listen. What is it?

Some sort of grumbling noise – like a giant machine working away in the depths of the refinery. Or perhaps it's an animal – a guard dog, growling in the shadows.

You creep forward.

At the far end of the corridor is another door. You can feel the door handle in the dark. And you can hear the low, rumbling growl from the other side.

It's definitely not machinery.

But what is it?

And do you dare open the door to find out?

If you want to open the door, risk your life on 51.

If you would prefer to go back and live another day, try 15.

'Maybe we should give it the benefit of the doubt,' you suggest.

The Doctor gives you a curious look, eyes twinkling. 'Well, you may be right. It's good to keep an open mind, and I admire your positive attitude. Let's say our crabby friend here is telling the truth. What then?'

You're not sure. It's Amy who comes up with an answer: 'We need to talk to the authorities — the people in charge of the refinery — for starters. They'll know.'

'Maybe they can give us more details of the Macra's plans,' you agree.

'Yeah, maybe,' nods the Doctor. He's far from convinced. But he turns back to the Macra. 'I'll switch off the oxygen. You've got two minutes to prove your case.'

He sonics the oxygen controls and the Macra lets out a throaty sigh of relief. 'Thank you,' it grumbles. 'Two minutes is all I need.'

A door opens and a squad of uniformed guards rush in, fanning out across the room. Each man bears the insignia of GasTech, the company that runs the refinery. Alarmingly, they are all armed with submachine guns.

The Doctor takes it in his stride, but his tone hardens. 'You may be helping the humans here,' he says to the Macra, 'but I don't think they'll be helping us.'

'How right you are, Doctor,' says the guard captain. He aims his sub-machine gun at your head.

Quick - you'd better get to 48.

Wisely, you decide to double-back – but it's not as simple as it seems. Very soon you're lost – all these corridors and tunnels look the same in the refinery and there doesn't seem to be anyone else around.

Eventually you find an exit door that leads to the outside.

You're standing beneath a huge gas silo. There are notices all around you alerting you to DANGEROUS SUBSTANCES and FLAMMABLE LIQUIDS. All around you can hear the sound of pumps and machinery and, in the distance, the noise of heavy gas tankers arriving and departing.

But which way back? Should you go back to the reception area and try to catch up with your school party?

If you want to head back to reception, go to 25.

If you would rather explore a bit further, go to 78.

You crack the code and data suddenly fills the screen, lighting up the Doctor's face.

'The Macra originally came to Earth by accident,' he says. 'Eggs attached to meteorites that fell into the Scapa Flow. Too cold for the Macra to hatch up there, but they were found by an oceanic research vessel owned by one of the umbrella companies that runs GasTech.'

'How did they know what they were?' you ask.

'They couldn't have known. They probably just looked liked lumps of rock. But perhaps someone was smart enough to realise that they weren't just lumps of rock. Or maybe it happened by accident – one of them hatched. Brought down to a warmer climate, maybe, subjected to various scientific prodding and poking. Who knows what might happen? But embryonic Macra develop extremely quickly – they are one of the universe's great survivors and adaptors. You should see what they look like in the year five billion. Make these guys look like shrimps.'

'Rather than crabs?' Amy asks mischievously.

'But look at this,' says the Doctor, pointing at the screen. 'Genetic scientists employed by GasTech made their own adaptations to the Macra genome. Successfully cloned a series of enhanced Macra – with highly developed intelligence.'

'Which is what I guess we saw,' you say.

'But why?' Amy wants to know.

'That's what we need to find out.'

'We should speak to the scientists on the lower levels,' you say.

'We could,' the Doctor agrees. 'Or we could stay put and ask one of the super-intelligent Macra.'

If you want to head down to the next level and ask the scientists first, go to 21.

If you want to question the Macra instead, go to 62.

You quickly follow the man into the next room.

It's some kind of antechamber, with a set of lift doors and a couple of other metal hatches. There's no furniture. It all looks very functional.

The man starts to use the metal instrument on one of the doors — it emits a high-pitched whine and the door opens with a heavy clunk to reveal the entrance to a large, circular pipe.

You can't help asking, 'How did you do that?'

Without even looking around, the man replies, 'Sonic screwdriver. Very useful for unlocking things that are locked. Question is — why was this door locked? Where does it lead?'

'Er...'

He looks around, finally, and glances at you with a pair of deep-set, intelligent eyes. 'Hi. I'm the Doctor. Have you seen Amy anywhere? Tall, red hair, short skirt — you can't miss her.'

'No,' you say.

'Pity. Lost her again. She will wander off. They all do, eventually.' He smiles briefly at you. 'I'll bet you'll wander off at some point too. You already have, after all.'

You glance guiltily back at the door you came through. On the other side of that is the reception area – and your school party.

'Still, we've more to think about than you,' the Doctor says, flipping his sonic screwdriver and catching it again. 'It's decision time, my friend. Do we stop and look for Amy – or do we investigate this interesting-looking pipe?'

If you want to find Amy first, look for her on 99.

If you think you'd better check the pipe, go straight to 107.

You head back to the refinery itself. The Doctor seems to know exactly where he's going!

A few seconds' work with the sonic screwdriver gains you entry. Inside, you follow the Doctor and Amy down a number of deserted corridors.

Deserted, that is, until a squad of guards appears from a side door. They are dressed in GasTech uniforms and – surprisingly – carry automatic pistols.

'Raise your hands,' advises the Doctor, 'slowly.'

'He doesn't like guns much,' Amy tells you as she raises her hands.

'It's not the guns so much as the people holding them,' corrects the Doctor. 'A gun is useless until someone pulls the trigger. Always look for the someone.'

You're holding your hands up. You don't want to take any chances.

'This is a secure area,' the guard says. 'No unauthorised personnel. You'd better come with us.'

He leads you to a very secure-looking door and ushers you all inside...

If you want to try and escape, make a dash for 104.

If you think you should do what the Doctor says and go quietly, try 95.

'Wait here,' advises the Doctor. 'We'll see what happens – we don't want them to notice us now!'

But it's too late – you *have* been noticed!

You hear a sound behind you – a soft, scuttling sound of something hard on the rock. All three of you turn slowly and see a group of Macra standing over you, eyes glimmering in the firelight, claws poised menacingly over your necks.

'Run!' screams the Doctor, without a second's hesitation.

You squirm from beneath the Macra and scatter. The Doctor runs left, you break right – and Amy takes the middle route. For a moment the Macra are thrown into confusion, tangling each other up with their legs and pincers in their haste to pursue.

The three of you head for the exit, scrambling back the way you came.

'There's too many of them!' gasps Amy. 'We'll never make it!'

'It's a proper infestation,' agrees the Doctor, still running. 'We need help – got to get outside.'

There's a mad dash for fresh air and you squeeze your way through narrow fissures in the rock until suddenly you emerge into cold daylight. You're almost laughing with relief, but the Doctor's already clicking his fingers for Amy's mobile phone.

'Time to put in a call,' he says grimly.

Who's he gonna call? Find out on 27.

The blue light is clearly unnatural. It comes from a series of fluorescent tubes arranged down the ceiling of a low, wide, underground workshop.

'This is more like it,' says the Doctor, rubbing his hands together like a proper science geek.

'Who'd build a lab this far below ground?' Amy wonders.

'Someone who didn't want it found very easily,' you suggest.

'That's right,' says the Doctor, scampering up and down the benches, examining equipment – oscilloscopes, electron microscopes, centrifuges, DNA extrapolators. 'Someone with something to hide.'

'Mad scientist?' queries Amy.

'Does it show?' smiles the Doctor, modestly.

'I mean – is that who built this place? Some sort of mad, freaky science guy experimenting on the Macra?'

'Or on human beings?' you wonder.

'Or both,' the Doctor adds. He points to a circular entrance in one wall – the start of some kind of pipeline. Above the entrance are the words:

NO ENTRY – EXPERIMENT Z

'I don't know about you two,' says the Doctor, 'but I just can't resist a notice that says "no entry"...'

Follow the Doctor to 118.

You go down several levels and then hurry through a network of laboratories and workshops until, at last, you find some other people.

'Hello, I'm the Doctor and these are my friends,' announces the Doctor as he bursts in. 'Cooperate and you'll all live – probably. Don't cooperate and you will all die – definitely.'

The collected scientists look at you all, dumbfounded.

'I'm taking that as a "cooperate",' smiles the Doctor.

'Are these the guys who've been experimenting on the Macra?' you ask.

'I don't think so,' murmurs the Doctor. 'I think these are more like gas engineers.'

'What's going on?' one of the scientists asks.

'Excellent question. The easy answer is this: an alien species known as the Macra has infiltrated the gas refinery. The Macra breathe toxic fumes – so they love it here. But they won't stop at the refinery. They'll find a way to pump out more and more toxic gas until it takes over the entire atmosphere of the planet – and then they'll take over Earth. Believe me, I've seen it happen. No more humans, plenty more Macra. Oh, and they look like giant crabs – *really* giant crabs – did I mention that?'

The scientists look even more dumbfounded.

'Did you say alien species?' repeats one of them, incredulously.

'Yeah, but really, that was the least important part.'

'You're mad. We're calling security!'

The Doctor rolls his eyes. 'Why can't they just believe me for once? Do I have a dishonest face or something?' He looks at you, his dark eyes glimmering deep in their sockets beneath the heavy fringe of dark hair. There's a strange smile on his lips and you find it a bit difficult to answer his question...

So don't hesitate any more – go straight to 43.

'This all stops here,' says the Doctor firmly.

The interior doors crash open and soldiers pour through – but these aren't GasTech security guards. They wear black uniforms and red berets with a winged insignia.

'Unified Intelligence Taskforce!' shouts the Doctor happily. 'UNIT for short! You had us all worried there, for a minute!'

The UNIT captain salutes smartly. 'You must be the Doctor,' he smiles. 'We were told you'd be here.'

The Doctor looks surprised. 'Really?'

'Well, it was termed a distinct possibility,' says the captain. He looks the Doctor up and down. 'Let's just say you fit the description.'

'Really?'

'And you can relax. We're here to take charge of the situation now...'

'Really?'

'Captain Grant,' the UNIT man introduces himself. 'I believe there's a problem with Macra here.'

'You're very well-informed,' says Amy.

'It's our job, miss. We've been monitoring the research and development centre at GasTech for some time. They've been importing Macra eggs and growing them in order to breathe the poisonous fumes the refinery produces as a by-product. It's a pretty crazy idea, but our scientific advisors say it could work.'

'Well, it could,' the Doctor agrees. 'But it would have to be managed very carefully.'

'That's why UNIT are here. We can't afford to let that kind of thing carry on in private business. It's best left to the professionals.'

'Quite.' The Doctor doesn't look too sure, but he's clearly relieved to see GasTech officials and security men being taken away by UNIT troopers.

'We'll deal with the remaining Macra and make sure the refinery is made properly safe,' says Captain Grant. 'But I'd appreciate it if you could do us one small favour, Doctor.'

'Such as?'

'Make sure no more Macra eggs reach Earth!'

The Doctor smiles. 'Of course I will. In fact, Amy and I will make it our number one priority. Come on, Miss Pond!'

Amy turns and smiles at you. 'Time for us to go, I'm afraid. You'll have quite a report to write up for your school trip.'

That's true – especially when you see the Doctor and Amy go inside the blue police box on the far side of the room. A moment later, it vanishes with a raucous noise. And it's like they've never been here...

THE END

You begin thrashing around on the table, calling the Macra every name you can think of – anything to distract it and to stop it noticing the Doctor and Amy!

You can see them creeping across the room. The Doctor starts working on some controls with the sonic screwdriver and suddenly the room is filled with a loud hissing noise.

The effect on the Macra is instant – it collapses backwards, choking and coughing, its legs waving madly in the air.

Amy unfastens the straps holding you down and you roll quickly off the table.

You're very grateful – another minute and you'd have been done for!

'What did you do to the Macra?' Amy asks the Doctor.

The Doctor watches the creature as it grows weaker and weaker. 'I've used the aircon system to fill the room with pure oxygen. It's poison to the Macra.'

'Will it die?' you ask.

'Not if I shut off the flow – but we'll have to leave straight away.'

'Then let's do it,' Amy says.

But the Doctor hesitates. 'If we go now we may lose the chance of finding out what's going on. There must be something here that can tell us.'

If you want to search the lab, go to 46.

If you think the Macra might have the answers, go to 64.

'The Macra are loose,' the scientist tells you.

'Well, duh!' retorts the Doctor. 'We can see that! The question is – how? Where did you get a swarm of Macra from? They're not usually found in this sector of the galaxy, let alone this planet!'

As he speaks, the Doctor uses the sonic screwdriver to herd the infant Macra to one side of the room.

'It's a long story,' the scientist replies. 'We had hoped to use them to help solve the problem of toxic fumes from the gas refinery...'

'It's a possibility,' muses the Doctor. 'But not really practicable. Baby Macra for industrial use? What will you do when the parents come calling?'

'They already have.'

The Doctor turns to you and Amy. 'We have to act quickly. Everyone here is in terrible danger.'

'How can we help?' you ask.

'We have to save the refinery and everyone in it – including your school party!'

If you want to try and help your school party first, go to 7.

If you think you should concentrate on the scientists, go to 56.

Heading back to the reception area, you find your way blocked by a series of chain-link fences. There are notices saying NO ADMITTANCE – TRESPASSERS WILL BE PROSECUTED.

Uh-oh – you've wandered into a restricted area.

But then you hear a strange wheezing and groaning noise... and something truly remarkable happens: a large blue box materialises out of thin air in front of you. It's got windows and a notice declaring POLICE BOX above two narrow doors.

Before you can react, the doors snap open and two people emerge – a man in a jacket and bow tie and lace-up boots, and a young woman in a short skirt.

'Hello!' says the man. 'I'm the Doctor and this is Amy. Can you direct us to the GasTech refinery?'

Stunned, you point behind them, where the refinery rises up into the sky like a giant, steel, industrial behemoth.

Then they see the "no admittance" signs. 'Well, we'll see about that!' the Doctor declares happily. 'There are two ways in as far as I'm concerned. We either go via the TARDIS...' He indicates the police box. 'Or we use my sonic screwdriver.' He holds up a slim, metallic device like a hi-tech wand.

If you want to go in the TARDIS, go to 70.

If you want him to use the sonic screwdriver, go to 85.

The beach is full of pebbles and seaweed. The surf looks cold and grey and unforgiving.

You walk along the beach a little way until you hear something move on the shingle behind you.

Turning around, the three of you watch a mound of pebbles rising up in the middle of the beach. Then, with an explosion of sand, something huge and red erupts from the ground.

'Macra!' yells the Doctor.

You can hardly believe your eyes – it's a giant crab all right, with huge claws and black eyes on the end of stalks. It heaves itself free of the sand and rocks and starts scuttling towards you.

'Run!'

You all hare off down the beach – but you're heading for the shoreline!

Splashing through the freezing surf, the three of you try to outrun the Macra. Even though it's got six legs, it's not very fast!

'We're trapped here,' realises the Doctor. 'We need to head back up – towards those caves!'

There are caves set in the cliff face – but can you make it in time?

You might be able to outrun the Macra and carry on along the beach on 76.

Or you can try and head for the cave on 69.

A short time later, black military helicopters are hovering over the main GasTech compound. Gunships circle the refinery. Ropes drop from the helicopters and UNIT troops begin rappelling down the lines to meet you.

The Doctor, bending low under the down-draught, rushes forward to meet the commanding officer.

'Captain Stone, at your disposal, sir.' The officer snaps to attention.

'Just call me Doctor.'

'What seems to be the problem, sir – I mean Doctor?'

'Macra infestation, right here, right now. The people in charge of this refinery are colluding with a race of giant crabs who want to suck in the poisonous fumes it creates for their own purposes. I need help to get them all under control – which is why I've called in UNIT. If you can help me get them into my TARDIS, I can take them off Earth for good.'

'Right, leave it with us, Doctor...'

'One thing,' the Doctor grabs Stone by the arm in a surprisingly strong grip. His eyes are serious. 'Minimal use of force. No unnecessary bloodshed. And I come along as scientific advisor.'

Join the attack on 106.

'That sounds too good to be true,' says the Doctor cautiously. He fixes the UNIT soldier with a penetrating stare. 'Is it?'

'We've been in negotiation with the Macra Controllers for months,' he says. 'They're willing to lend us drone Macra to deal with the toxic fumes. If this deal works, GasTech will lead the way in providing cheap, clean energy.'

'Clean because the Macra have kindly offered to clean it up for you,' the Doctor points out.

'But they benefit too. They're running out of the gas they need on their planet in the Andromeda Galaxy. Without the GasTech by-products, they'll die.'

'OK,' nods the Doctor. 'It sounds good – but I need to check the refinery out to make sure it's all safe. The Macra can be tricky. Believe me, I've dealt with them before.'

'I take it you are the man they call "the Doctor", sir,' smiles the soldier.

'That's right!'

'Malcolm sends his regards.'

The Doctor's eyebrows shoot up. 'I can see my reputation goes before me, as usual.'

'It does indeed.' The UNIT trooper shakes the Doctor's hand. 'I'm

Lieutenant Harper; pleased to meet you. I've read your file. You travel around in time and space in an old police box and don't like being saluted. You prefer to be addressed as "Doctor" rather than "sir" or even "doc" and you're often in the company of a beautiful woman.'

Amy smiles, almost blushing, as Lt Harper gives her a dashing smile.

'All right, Harper,' says the Doctor. 'Get your mind back on the job.

'Roger that.' He nods briskly, sparing a wink for Amy. 'We'll take you back to the refinery and you can speak to the Macra Controllers yourself, Doctor.'

Go to 44.

You follow the Doctor into a gloomy chamber.

Suddenly a light snaps on — for a second you're dazzled.

But then you see you are standing in a laboratory of some sort — full of benches and test tubes bubbling away.

And right in front of you is a phalanx of armed guards in black uniforms bearing the GasTech Security insignia.

'Wondered when we'd get to the firearms,' sighed the Doctor.

The leader of the guards points an automatic pistol at the Doctor. 'You're trespassing, sir,' he says.

'Sorry, don't talk to people with guns — it's a matter of principle,' the Doctor replies. 'I'm looking for — Amy!'

The guards have shoved a young woman into view. She's a stunning redhead in a short skirt. She looks scared but defiant. 'Hey,' she says to the Doctor. 'What took you so long?'

The guards have her covered and the automatic is still aimed at the Doctor, but he doesn't seem to notice. 'Good to see you again, Amy. Find any aliens?'

Before she can reply, the guard captain rests the muzzle of his pistol against the Doctor's head.

They've got the Doctor and Amy covered. But no one seems to have taken you into account.

So...

If you want to make a break for it now, dash to 104.

If you'd rather not risk a bullet, hold your hands up on 48.

'We ought to find out what the Macra are up to,' says the Doctor. And he heads down the tunnel.

It heads at an angle downwards — by your estimation, you are soon underground. You can hear the machinery of the gasworks thrumming through the walls as you go.

'So where are you from?' you ask Amy.

'I'm from Scotland.'

'And the Doctor?'

'He's from another planet.'

'Right.'

'No, seriously. He travels through space and time in an old police box called the TARDIS.'

'An old police box?'

'Yeah. It's bigger on the inside than the outside.'

You could be in the company of a pair of lunatics — but there's something about them, something reassuring. Something you feel, almost instinctively, that you can trust.

But it's starting to get cold down here — and the walls of the tunnel are covered in condensation. Soon you are all shivering and damp.

Eventually the Doctor calls a halt. He's found something interesting, and he's almost hopping from foot to foot with excitement. 'Look at this!'

There's a wide metal grille in the floor of the duct. Beyond it is a hatchway leading to — who knows where?

The Doctor opens the hatch a crack. 'We've come out near the coast! The refinery was built by the sea so that there was a ready supply of cold water to help cool the fuel pumps. This outlet must lead to the beach...'

'But what about this?' Amy asks, pointing down through the grille. Beneath, a dim green light is shining. It certainly looks peculiar, and the Doctor's attention is easily drawn to it.

If you want to go outside and investigate the coastal areas, go through the door to 76.

If you want to see what lies beneath the ducting, go through the grille to 41.

'I'm not about to kill anyone,' the Doctor says. But there is a look on his face that chills you to the bone – because you know that this admission will give the Macra victory.

Already, the terrifying beast is rearing up on its crab-like legs with a triumphant hiss, ready to attack.

'Look out!' you cry, dragging Amy to one side as a massive claw snaps forward.

In seconds there is pandemonium – the school kids are racing for the exit. Everyone is diving out of reach of those deadly claws.

Snap! You manage to duck at the last moment, but you feel the swipe of the claws through your hair. Your blood runs cold with a sudden fear of death. How did you ever get into this situation?

The Macra continues to attack in a frenzy, and its horrible shrieks of rage are awful to hear. You can see the Doctor is pinned to the floor by one of its many legs, but as you move to help – disaster!

Thud!

Something heavy and hard – a claw? – catches you a glancing blow on the back of the head.

And you black out...

Wake up on 93!

You're given a lift back to the main entrance of the refinery in a UNIT hovercraft. It floats up the beach and zooms across the grassland and car parks until it reaches the entrance to the Control Tower.

There are a number of UNIT helicopters and troop carriers waiting outside the refinery. And, marching sideways out of the entrance with their claws held high, are a column of Macra under guard.

You're led past the UNIT troopers, armed with heavy weaponry. The UNIT commander indicates a large machine gun hefted by one of the nearby soldiers. 'Adapted from a Heckler & Koch G3 assault rifle, loaded with armour-piercing depleted Uranium rounds designed to penetrate Sontaran armour. Those things will get through Macra shell no problem.'

'Boys' toys,' muses the Doctor. He doesn't look impressed.

But it's good to see the Macra being led away and the refinery being cleared.

'What about the GasTech executives who were in collusion with the Macra?' Amy asks. 'There must have been a few board members in on the deal, after all.'

'We've rounded them up and taken them to a secure facility for questioning. Turns out they were using stolen teleport technology to beam the Macra in.'

'And you're going to use the same technology to beam them right back where they came from, I trust?' enquires the Doctor, his eyes boring into those of the UNIT commander.

'Absolutely.'

'See that you do – or I'll be back, asking some difficult questions.'

'Understood, Doctor.'

The Macra are being held in electrified pens on the perimeter of the refinery. Apparently satisfied, the Doctor takes you into the reception area, where your school party are waiting.

'We've been looking everywhere for you – and then these soldiers turn up and the whole trip turns into a disaster!' exclaims one of the teachers. 'Where have you been?'

'I got lost,' you tell him simply. You see the Doctor and Amy going into the old blue police box – and seconds later it fades from view. 'Why?' you ask the teacher. 'What have I missed?'

THE END

'You can't be serious,' says the Doctor. 'The Macra are a hostile alien life form. They invade any planet they can get their claws on. They're the Scourge of the Galaxy.'

'They are here to help us, Doctor.'

'I very much doubt it!' The Doctor shakes his head in exasperation. 'I never thought I'd see the day when UNIT started cosying up to aliens.'

'Then you won't help us?' The UNIT man's gaze hardens.

But the Doctor's gaze is like ice. 'I'll do everything in my power to stop you.'

At a signal from the UNIT soldier, several troopers move in to arrest the Doctor. You and Amy are held at gunpoint too.

'You've got this all wrong,' the Doctor tells the UNIT men. 'I'm the Doctor! Check with Headquarters in Geneva. They'll tell you to listen to me!'

'I might just do that, sir,' says the UNIT soldier. 'But until then I can't take the risk of you interfering.'

'But interfering is what I do best!'

But his protests fall on deaf ears. You are led underground and marched along a corridor that you are informed runs right under the ocean bed, and back towards the refinery.

'Where we started,' Amy notes.

The three of you are pushed into a small, bare concrete room with a dark pool of water at its centre.

What's happening? Find out on 95.

'Down!' shouts the Doctor. 'Down, down, down!'

You and Amy head into the lower tunnel, running as fast as you can down the incline. You can hear the Doctor's boots pounding behind you.

It's getting darker and colder, and the rock is more slippery. You have to slow down. Eventually, you find yourselves in complete and utter darkness.

The Doctor switches on his pen-torch. The little light illuminates your faces – but that's about all. 'We can't pause for too long,' the Doctor whispers. 'The Macra will be right behind us.'

'But what can we do?' wonders Amy. 'We can't see a thing and I think the tunnel's getting narrower.'

And she's right. Any progress will have to be made centimetres at a time – your clothes and shoulders keep getting snagged on jagged rocks, and you can't see more than a hand's distance in front of you. It's terrifyingly claustrophobic.

And now you can hear the rattle and clatter of the Macra approaching down the tunnel behind you. But you won't see them. It's too dark.

If you want to press on and hope the tunnel widens, squeeze through to 81.

If you think the Doctor should come up with a clever idea, go to 124.

'Shouldn't we try to stop it?' you ask as the teleport hum fills the air and a shape starts to appear in the middle of the chamber.

The Doctor's already sonicing the control panel. 'I'm trying to reverse the polarity – send whatever it is back to wherever it's coming from!'

But Mr Jones, the school teacher, suddenly steps forward and snatches the sonic screwdriver out of the Doctor's hand, pushing him roughly aside. 'I can't allow you to do that,' says Mr Jones. There is an odd light in his eyes – as if he's not quite himself. Even more oddly, he begins to operate the controls on the teleport panel – as if he knows exactly what to do!

'What's happening?' asks Amy. 'How does he know how to do that?'

'Some kind of mind control,' says the Doctor. 'He's under alien influence!'

The teleport crackles loudly as a shape materialises in the middle of the chamber – a huge, crab-like creature with enormous claws and black eyes on stalks. It quivers and snarls as the Doctor steps up.

'The Macra,' he says. 'I thought as much – the shell architecture, the mind control, the fondness for gas... but teleport technology? Aren't you over-reaching yourselves a bit?'

'It is time for the Macra to assume control of this world,' announces the alien creature in a deep, bubbling voice.

'You can't control the minds of everyone on the planet.'

Mr Jones is rubbing his eyes, back to his normal self as the Macra's grip on his mind is released.

'We used weak minds to secure a bridgehead,' explains the Macra. 'To help design and build this refinery.'

'But why?' you ask.

'We will use this refinery to flood the Earth's atmosphere with gases that are poisonous to humans and animals – but perfect for the Macra Horde!'

Hurry to 116.

'I'll let you help Earth on one condition,' says the Doctor.

The Macra clicks its claws impatiently. 'On whose authority do you speak?' 'Well, my own, of course. But I also speak for the people around me. This is their world — not yours. You can stay and help, by all means, because the humans here seem incapable of looking after their own planet sensibly. They're very reliant on fossil fuels at the moment, and so I'm sure a bit of help with the by-products would be appreciated.'

'We can serve each other,' insists the Macra. 'We will consume the toxic fumes and leave the humans to live their lives in peace.'

'For now,' the Doctor replies. 'But it can't continue indefinitely. There are other worlds with atmospheres that would kill human beings but be perfect for you.'

'Until we find a suitable planet, then.'

'That's right. And while you're here, make sure no toxic gases are leaking. There was quite a pong back there.'

'We will deal with that immediately.'

'And only enough Macra to serve this refinery,' the Doctor adds warningly. 'That's your limit.'

'Of course.'

'Can we trust them?' asks Amy.

'Not all alien life-forms are invaders,' the Doctor smiles. 'There's good Macra and bad Macra, just like there are good and bad humans. You're lucky — this one and his friends are here for a bit of mutual help.'

He turns back to you. 'It's time for us to leave. Amy and I will have a quiet word with the authorities here and make sure everything goes smoothly. You'd better get your school party back to the reception area and start again.'

And that sounds like a good idea!

THE END

37

'Check the Doctor's all right,' you say. 'I'll distract the Macra!'

You pick up the Doctor's torch and start waving the light around in front of the giant crab. It hisses in fury, trying to catch the dazzling light in its huge claws.

Amy kneels down by the Doctor. 'He's out cold!'

And suddenly there are other people in the room — soldiers with guns, opening fire on the huge monster in the shadows. Automatic gunfire crackles loudly in the confined chamber, bullets splintering the thick shell around the creature's mouth.

The Macra retreats, squealing furiously. Its pincers snap and crack and flail around, but the soldier's firepower overwhelms it.

You take your chance and get out of the chamber. There are other men with the soldiers — scientists and executives from the gas company. They help Amy take the Doctor to a chair, where someone brings him a glass of water.

The soldiers have closed the heavy door on the Macra, and the sounds of its fury can no longer be heard.

Go to 108.

Immediately you help the Doctor turn the large metal wheel anti-clockwise. It's stiff but it turns.

'Hurry!' says Amy. 'They're getting restless!'

Gradually the valve turns and the gas flow is cut off!

The response is surprisingly rapid – the Macra around the altar start panicking, choking and gasping. The beast on the dais rears up, its great claws scraping on the stonework.

'They're weakening already,' the Doctor notes with satisfaction.

Soon the Macra in the cavern have all but succumbed. Leaving them dormant, you quickly find your way back up to the refinery – where the situation is being repeated. Any Macra present in the gasworks are also choking and struggling.

The Doctor gets hold of the refinery bosses in very short order – and tells them exactly how to return the dormant monsters to the planet they came from.

'I've given them a one-way teleport control programmed into the Macra genome,' the Doctor tells you. 'Should be easy – the hard part will be rounding up all the dormant Macra.'

'At least they won't put up much resistance,' says Amy.

'And the refinery will have to seriously rethink its clean energy policy,' the Doctor says. 'No more shortcuts using hostile aliens!'

The Doctor and Amy are soon standing by the old police box, ready to leave. It's been quite a day for you – but do you want it to end? After all, the Doctor and Amy are bound to have plenty more adventures...

Do you want to go with them or stay behind? You decide!

THE END

'There will be guards in the research area,' says the Doctor. 'Let's just see what's through here...'

He leads the way into the next ventilation shaft. It travels horizontally across the refinery in a zigzag, winding its way through the gas pipes and silos. Bent double, the three of you make your way along the steel tunnel, your footsteps echoing wildly.

The tunnel takes a turn upwards – you have to crawl up at a 45 degree angle. It's difficult, because the metal surface is quite slippery. But eventually you reach the top.

The shaft ends in a ventilation grille, which the Doctor removes with the aid of his sonic screwdriver.

There's a sharp wind blowing as you emerge – looking out over the rest of the refinery. You're on some kind of gantry next to the top of one of the largest silos. The view is quite breathtaking – not only of all the gantries below, but the giant Macra squatting on top of the nearby silo!

With a scream, it rises on its six spindly legs and reaches out with its pincers. Its arms seem unnaturally long and fearsome – and there's nowhere to run to!

You can stay and fight on 121.

Or you can try and jump down to the next gantry on 129.

Amy turns the professor over as best she can as the speedboat bounces across the waves. 'I think he's dead!'

The Doctor leaves the controls of the powerboat to you and examines the old man. 'Heart attack. Poor old fool.'

'Doctor!' Amy cries, seeing something over his shoulder – behind the boat.

You turn around to see what she's pointing at.

The sea is foaming alongside the powerboat – a fountain of water suddenly erupting around a huge, reddish shape emerging from the surf.

'Macra!' screams Amy.

You haul the wheel to port, steering the boat away from the marauding crab. The Doctor and Amy fall sideways as the boat leans to. The Macra's claws snap in the air behind the vessel.

Another bursts out of the water nearby and you swing the boat the other way. It's like a fairground ride as the ship swings from side to side, evading a herd of giant Macra.

'How come they're so fast in the water?' you want to know.

'Who cares!' yells Amy. 'Just drive the boat!'

'Pilot the boat!' corrects the Doctor. 'You pilot a boat!'

'We can't outrun them!' you yell. 'There's too many!

'We'll have to stand and fight,' shouts the Doctor grimly. The sea spray has made his hair stand out from his head in a wild tangle of black. His eyes shine with the light of adventure.

'How?' yells Amy.

If you want to search the speedboat for something to use as a weapon, try 117.

If you think you should try and outrun the Macra, accelerate to 47.

The Doctor gets through the grille using his sonic screwdriver, and then drops down through the hole. His boots hit the deck below with a loud, reverberating clang. 'Come on down!' he calls back up. 'The green light's lovely.'

Actually, you don't find the green light lovely at all. It's weird and sinister and alien. And there is a persistent throbbing noise like a huge, diseased heartbeat.

'So where does this lead?' asks Amy.

'Not a clue,' replies the Doctor. 'That's what we're trying to find out. Onwards and downwards!'

'Hang on,' you say. 'What's that horrible smell?'

The Doctor sniffs the air — and his eyes go wide with alarm. Immediately he delves in a pocket and produces three identical, spotless white handkerchiefs. He hands one to you, one to Amy, and then clamps the third over his mouth and nose. 'Mmmph mmph mmmph!' he says.

'Pardon?'

He takes the hanky away from his mouth for a second. 'I said poison gas!'

Quickly you cover your mouth and nose with the hanky, trying not to breathe. You're already feeling dizzy and Amy looks sick.

'This way!' yells the Doctor, darting forward. 'He points at the floor. 'Down again, I'm afraid — there's a hole in the floor here with a ladder leading down. Some kind of ventilation shaft, perhaps!' He's coughing and choking and can't really speak anymore.

But you've spotted something else — the tunnel you're in leads away to the left. You can't see around the corner but it might be an escape route!

If you want to go down the shaft in the floor, go to 49.

If you want to see what's around the left turn, go to 82.

You quietly cross the room to take a closer look at the police box. It's tall, a deep blue colour, and apparently made from wood. But it's warm to the touch and humming gently, as if there's some kind of powerful machinery hidden away inside. You try the door but it's locked.

Slowly, you walk around the police box. There's no other way in and the windows are just too high for you to peek inside.

As you complete a circuit of the box you bump into a tall, red-haired girl in a mini skirt. She smiles brightly at you, excuses herself, and slips away.

But where did she come from? There's only one explanation – she must have been inside the police box! You try the doors again but it's still locked.

The girl hurries across the room and disappears through the same door as the man in the tweed jacket.

This is too intriguing!

You're about to follow the girl when you hear a noise behind you. There's some kind of rattling coming from the other side of the police box. Checking behind it, you find a door in the wall of the room that you hadn't noticed before.

There's a strange noise coming from the other side. It sounds like an animal – something grunting and snarling...

And it doesn't sound very friendly...

If you want to follow the red-haired girl, hurry across to 4.

If you want to find out what's making the noise behind the door, check out 66.

43

Suddenly the Doctor is galvanised into action. He vaults a nearby computer workstation, and in the confusion that follows, you follow him out of the lab. You run at breakneck speed through the refinery. 'What's the plan now?' Amy asks.

'We need to contact the authorities,' says the Doctor. 'This whole operation is out of control. We can't allow the Macra to take over. The refinery needs closing down — permanently. And I know just the people to do it.'

Once clear of the main building, the Doctor asks Amy for her mobile. He takes it, makes a quick adjustment with the sonic screwdriver, and then dials a number.

'Hello? Never mind all that security claptrap — this is an emergency. Put me through to Brigadier Lethbridge-Stewart immediately.'

'Who are you calling?' you ask.

'UNIT,' says the Doctor. 'Unified Intelligence Taskforce.' Suddenly he's talking on the phone again: 'What d'you mean, he's retired? Oh, I see. Wrong time frame. All right, then, try Captain Erisa Magambo. And it's still an emergency. What d'you mean, she's on holiday? Since when did UNIT take holidays? Wait a minute — do you know who I am? It's the Doctor!' He cups a hand over the phone and winks. 'That'll get 'em moving.'

'He knows all the right people,' smiles Amy.

The Doctor shushes her. 'Hello? Yes, that's right. The Doctor. Good. At last. Emergency 7 protocols — under authorisation code Delta Nine. GasTech oil refinery — Macra infiltration.'

What's going to happen next? Click on box E on screen and enter code word UNIT.

Or go straight to 27!

Lt Harper takes you to a small base on the island where a UNIT helicopter awaits. You accompany him, the Doctor and Amy in the chopper back to the mainland, landing in the middle of the refinery.

The Doctor is taken to the Control Tower. Your school party watches in amazement as you are led into a private room with the company executives and a couple of UNIT officers.

On a holographic screen in the centre of the control room is the image of a giant Macra – huge, with a gnarled shell and only one eye on the end of a stalk.

'Welcome, Doctor!' it says in a gurgling, alien voice.

'Hello there,' replies the Doctor, slipping into a seat and putting his hands behind his head. 'I'm told you're here to save the world.'

'We are the Macra Controllers – leaders of the Macra race. Many of our people are dying, Doctor – starved without access to the gases we need to live. This refinery produces exactly the gas we need to survive – by consuming the gas, we can help it provide clean, safe fuel for Earth.'

'No plans for invasion, then?'

'We wish to live in peace and harmony. We will supply only drone Macra to feed on the gas – they have no intelligence and cannot be a threat. We Controllers will be able to live on what little gas we have here on this planet.'

'That's very considerate of you.' The Doctor and UNIT go through the details of the plan very carefully. Safeguards are put in place to ensure that GasTech fulfils its side of the bargain – and the Macra theirs. UNIT will provide the security and, if the facility succeeds, it could open up a whole new era of human-alien cooperation.

The Doctor, satisfied with the result, slips out with Amy, leaving the UNIT people and the GasTech execs to go over the fine print.

You catch them up in the reception area, by the police box. Their spaceship.

'TARDIS,' says Amy. 'Stands for Time And Relative Dimension In Space. We can go anywhere in time and space. Want to come?'

You're not sure. You look back at your school party. It's been quite an adventure. Do you stay – or do you go?

Your choice – your destiny!

THE END

Immediately, GasTech men swarm around the burning Macra with fire extinguishers. The sizzling hulk is obscured by a cloud of CO_2 and the flames wither and die.

Climbing down from the gantry, the Doctor looks sadly at the charred remains. 'What a terrible waste...'

'We had to fight,' Amy reminds him. 'It was going to kill us.'

'What about all the other Macra?' you ask.

A GasTech man steps forward. 'We've taken control of the refinery. The guards that have been in collusion with the Macra have been arrested and confined to quarters. The rest of us are making our way through the refinery armed with flame-throwers.'

'A pretty brutal way to finish this business,' mutters the Doctor. He's still staring at the Macra corpse.

'There's no other way. The Macra were growing too strong.'

Amy sighs. 'It's a pity. It was a good idea, in a way, letting them consume the poison gas...'

'But too risky,' the Doctor tells her. 'You've seen what they're like. Allow them to get a foothold here, and they will spread all over Earth. That can't be allowed to happen.'

You can hear the roar of flame throwers around the refinery.

'What next?' You wonder.

'Back to where you started,' says the Doctor with a slight smile. 'Back to where we started. Our job here is done — but there are always other places to go, people to meet, adventures to be had.'

THE END

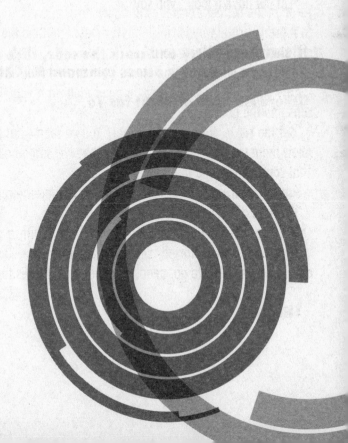

'We've no time to lose,' the Doctor says. 'We won't find out anything from this specimen. But there must be something here that can help.'

You search the laboratory, stepping carefully over the wheezing form of the Macra. Amy finds a computer workstation and punches up a series of screens that the Doctor finds very interesting.

He scans the data quickly – much more quickly than you can follow.

'This looks like some sort of database for the Macra experiment,' he says. 'But it's locked by a security code.'

'Let me have a look,' you say.

If you want to try and crack the code, click on box B on screen and enter access command MACRA CODE.

Otherwise head straight for 16.

'We'll never outrun them,' you yell, spitting out seawater. The speedboat bucks and twists over the waves, dodging in and out of the rampaging Macra.

'Push the boat as fast as you can,' the Doctor tells you. 'Full throttle!'

You push the accelerator right down and the boat surges forward with a scream of its outboard engine. The prow of the boat tips up in the air and a great fan of water sprays out from the rear. A Macra flashes past in a blur of red shell.

'They're still gaining on us!' shouts Amy.

The Doctor thrusts his sonic screwdriver into the boat's outboard and a green glow flashes. The speedboat lurches forward again, practically flying over the waves. As the vessel rocks, Professor Greif's body is accidentally tipped overboard.

'The professor!' shouts Amy.

'It's too late now!' cries the Doctor.

You twist around to look back. The Macra converge on the body in the water, snapping and tearing and dragging it under the waves.

'He helped us again, even in death,' the Doctor notes.

The powerboat starts to lose speed as the engine coughs and splutters.

'The engine's burnt out!' says the Doctor. 'Head back to the shore.'

You steer the boat towards the distant beach and dry land. The Macra are still thrashing around in the sea as the three of you scramble up the beach...

Go to 76.

Slowly, you raise your hands.

You are all marched at gunpoint to a low-ceilinged room deep underground. You can hear the heavy machinery of the refinery grinding away above your heads, transmitted through metres of concrete.

The floor of the chamber slopes down into a pool of murky water. At the far end of the pool is a wide metal grille, and beyond that — blackness.

'What is this place?' asks Amy.

'It's not the guest suite, that's for sure,' the Doctor comments.

'I've got orders from Mr Quipe to leave you here,' the guard captain says.

'Then leave us here,' the Doctor shrugs. 'We prefer each other's company.'

The guard laughs chillingly. 'Yeah, right.'

And then he closes the door behind him with a loud, echoing clang.

Go to 95.

'We go that way,' says the Doctor, pointing downwards. 'Deep. Dark. Damp. That's where the nasties always are.'

'And that's what we're looking for?' you ask.

'That's what I'm always looking for,' replies the Doctor.

You all climb into the hole in the ground and start down the ladder. It's cold and hard going, and gets darker with every step. The sounds of your hands and feet scraping on the metal rungs echoes up and down the shaft.

Eventually you reach the bottom. You're standing in another tunnel, deep underground, with metal walls all rusted and studded with iron rivets. The Doctor has already moved on, sniffing the air. 'Smell's getting stronger,' he says.

You follow him through a narrow doorway into a huge open space. It's a cavern — immense and vaulted with giant stalactites and rock formations.

'This way!' The Doctor's already bounding off through the cave, dodging around the rocks.

'Is it always like this with him?' you ask Amy.

'Yep!'

The Doctor's reached an intersection in the cave. A flickering orange light shines from one cave entrance — and a bright, brilliant blue glow shines from the other.

'Which way?' wonders Amy.

If the Doctor wants to investigate the cave with the blue light, go to 20.

If you take charge to investigate the cave with the flickering light, go to 61.

You slip quietly through the door. No one has noticed.

You don't intend to be long – this is just a quick look around, nothing more.

You're in a short corridor. It's brightly lit, but featureless. There's a strange antiseptic smell in the air, like a hospital, and the floor is made from rubberised tiles. It looks strangely futuristic and a little bit scary. But then this is a brand new gas refinery, that's why your school have come on a trip here – to find out how modern science is coping with the energy shortage, and what can be done to process gas and oil safely and efficiently. It's not a bad project really.

In fact, you can hear the distant sound of the refinery in operation – the low hum of machinery and computers, and you can even feel it through your trainers: a faint vibration.

There's no one about, so you venture a little further.

At the far end of the corridor is a junction with two doors. One is marked with a red triangle, and the other is marked with a green triangle. There is no writing on either and although they are closed they don't appear to be locked.

Surely a quick look behind one of the doors couldn't do any harm?

But which?

If you choose to go through the red door, go to 72.

If you want to try the green door, go to 13.

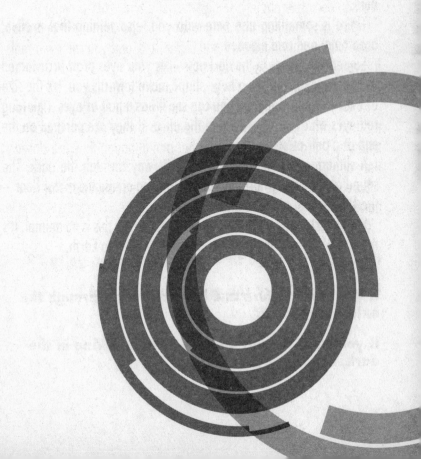

You push the door open. It leads into a large, echoing metal chamber. It's very dark, and there's a strange, musty smell in here – and something else, something that smells like gas.

Which is probably only to be expected in a gasworks.

You go into the room. Your footsteps echo hollowly on the metal floor. It feels oily underfoot – almost slimy. You dread to think what kind of algae is spread across the ground.

But the grumbling noise is louder.

And suddenly you sense that you are not alone in this dark, echoing void.

There is something else here with you – something that is alive, breathing, and cold blooded.

Something moves in the darkness – as your eyes grow accustomed to the shadows, you see a huge shape move towards you. It's the size of a large van – and then you can see it has a pair of eyes... glowing red eyes which move around in the air as if they are perched on the end of a pair of stalks.

A slithering, scraping noise makes its way through the dark. The sound of something hard and heavy moving across the metal floor – the footsteps of many inhuman legs.

Your heart is pounding in your chest. You know this is no animal. It's the size of an elephant but it is completely alien to Earth...

If you want to turn and head out back through the exit, hurry to 15.

If you want to wait and see what's lurking in the dark, head for 65.

'Try clockwise first,' says the Doctor.

The wheel turns easily. 'Is it having any affect?' you wonder.

Amy peers back at the fire-lit Macra. They are waving their claws in the flickering glow of the altar, chanting in their strange, guttural language. The great monster on the dais gives a savage roar of exultation.

'It's making them stronger!' Amy shouts.

The Doctor's eyes widen. 'Oh no – we've increased the gas flow!'

'We've made things worse!' you realise.

Soon the poison gas has filled the cavern and you can feel yourself losing consciousness.

The last thing you see before you collapse is the Macra, peering down at you with those inscrutable black eyes...

Wake up on 142.

Gas is pouring through the pipe. Amy's collapsing against the wall, coughing and heaving.

'We've got to open the hatch!' declares the Doctor. He's covered his mouth and nose with a large white handkerchief, but in his other hand is the sonic screwdriver.

He kneels down in front of the hatch and tries the screwdriver. It emits a shrill whine but nothing much seems to happen. Your eyes are watering and your head is swimming. You've got to get that door open soon or you'll pass out.

The Doctor adjusts the screwdriver and tries again. A different noise, but the same lack of effect.

'What's wrong with it?' you ask, coughing heavily.

'This door's been locked using old-fashioned bolts,' the Doctor says. He sounds peeved. 'Why couldn't they use a simple electronic code lock or a magnetic seal?'

He adjusts the screwdriver again and gets to work, but it's no use. The screwdriver slips out of his fingers as the gas begins to overwhelm him.

Amy is sliding down the wall, barely conscious. You can hardly see for the gas now as it fills the silo. You dare not draw another breath. Desperately, you start to pound on the metal wall of the silo, growing weaker by the second.

Clunk! Clunk! The sound of the bolts being drawn on the other side of the door is one of the sweetest things you've ever heard. The hatch swings open and you fling yourself out into the fresh air, gasping for breath. The Doctor follows you out with Amy.

One of the teachers from your school party, Mr Jones, is helping you to your feet. The school group is gathered all around.

'What's going on?' Mr Jones demands to know. 'We heard the banging and unlocked the hatch — but what are you all doing in there?'

'No time to explain,' says the Doctor. He's already hurrying past with Amy in tow. The Doctor turns to you as he goes, yelling, 'Stay here! Stick with the school party and stay out of trouble!'

If you think you should stay with the school party, stick to 112.

If you want to follow the Doctor and Amy, scoot along to 12.

The Doctor is clearly very angry — and he expresses this in a controlled, furious quietness. His lips set in a thin line, he simply turns towards the exit.

'Come on — we're leaving.'

'What are you intending to do, Doctor?' asks Quipe.

'Save lives,' the Doctor replies tersely.

Outside, he takes a deep breath of fresh air and closes his eyes. When they snap open again, they are full of purpose.

'Right — we've two options here,' he announces. 'Either we double back to the reception area and make sure everyone is safe first — including your school party,' he adds, glancing in your direction.

'Or?' prompts Amy.

'Or we follow that Macra over there.'

He's pointing behind you and Amy. You both whirl around to see the rear legs of a giant Macra disappearing around the next silo. It must have been creeping by very quietly.

'Perhaps it's injured?' suggests Amy.

'Or perhaps it just didn't want to be seen,' you add.

'Either way, the only chance of finding out is if we follow it,' says the Doctor. 'So which is it to be?'

If you want to rescue your school party, go to 7.

If you want to follow the Macra, go to 8.

The Doctor helps the professor sit up – but it's a serious blow. 'He's out cold.'

You manage to carry the old man together, manoeuvring him out of the door as the Macra flings aside the experiment table.

'Quick!' urges Amy.

You stagger out into the next room, but it's too late for the professor.

'He's dead,' the Doctor announces grimly. 'The Macra killed him – fractured skull by the looks of it.'

You lay the old man down gently, but there's no time for sentiment. The Macra is breaking out of the lab, roaring angrily.

'Where now?' you wonder.

'Lift!' says Amy, dragging you across the corridor to a pair of double doors. The Doctor's sonic screwdriver makes quick work of any security clearance and the doors hum open. The three of you pile inside and the doors slide shut on the advancing Macra. Its claws beat heavily on the metal, leaving huge dents, as the Doctor examines the controls.

'Up or down?' he asks.

'If we go up we'll run straight into refinery guards,' Amy points out.

'But we've no idea what's on the lower levels,' you say.

The Doctor looks from one to the other. 'Well, what's it to be?'

Head up to 5.

Or go down to 21.

'Let's concentrate on the here and now, though,' advises the Doctor. He ticks off points on his long fingers: 'One – we have the scientists here. Two – if we save the refinery, we save everyone. Three – the Macra depend on the poison gas this place produces. Four – erm...'

'Four – you need to stop the poison gas!' you say.

'Exactly! Stop the gas, stop the Macra.' He whirls around to address the scientists. 'Where are the gas controls?'

The Doctor is shown a number of large metal rings – keys for the valves which control the gas flow through the refinery. He starts to turn the first one – but it's heavy and very stiff.

Suddenly, something starts banging on the other side of the doors.

'Doctor!' Amy shouts. 'It's the Macra – they're trying to get in!'

'They must have realised what we're trying to do,' you say.

The Doctor's gritting his teeth with the exertion of trying to turn the wheels. 'Can't someone give me a hand?'

Amy's heading for the door. It's already buckling under the onslaught of the Macra. 'Someone help me make a barricade,' she says. 'We've got to keep them out!'

If you want to help Amy keep the Macra out, go to 111.

If you want to help the Doctor turn the gas off, go to 131.

'They're almost on us!' you scream.

Amy covers her face as the Macra swarm up the ramp. The Doctor works feverishly at the lock with his sonic screwdriver, but it's no use. The Macra are already clambering over your feet.

Suddenly the door hisses up and a figure in a white coat beckons you through.

You pile out of the chamber, the Macra scrabbling at your toes.

'Quickly! Close the door!'

The scientist tries to slam the door shut, but it's too late! Hundreds of the crabs have crawled through the gap and some of them stick to your clothes, holding on with their pincers.

'Get them off me!' yells Amy.

The Doctor uses his sonic screwdriver on the infant Macra, and one by one they fall away. But many of them continue scuttling around the room.

'This could be a problem,' sighs the Doctor.

'It is a problem!' replies the scientist.

Find out how big a problem it is on 24.

'Doctor! Amy!' Get out of here! Save yourselves!' you yell. You're scared, but you don't want them to face the same fate as this.

But the Doctor and Amy have other plans. Amy runs across the operating room, waving her arms madly at the Macra. The giant crab creature hisses angrily, lashing out with its huge claws. It's so bulky it finds it hard to move around the room, and Amy keeps out of harm's way.

The Doctor, meanwhile, has unfastened your bonds using the sonic screwdriver. He helps you off the operating table and together you head for the exit.

Amy ducks under the Macra's claw and joins you at the door. One quick blast with the sonic screwdriver and you're through!

'You were lucky,' the Doctor tells you. 'That Macra was about to operate on you.'

'What for?'

'No idea — yet. But I bet it wasn't for anything pleasant.' The Doctor leads you down a long corridor until you reach another exit. 'This should get us back to the reception area. You can rejoin your school party — it's too dangerous for you here.'

Before you can argue, the Doctor sonics the door and it slides open to reveal a guard in a company uniform carrying a gun.

He gives you a nasty smile and aims the pistol at your head...

Go to 48.

The Doctor trains the sonic screwdriver on the advancing Macra – but with little effect. He works desperately through the different settings but nothing seems to work.

'I can't find the right frequency!' he grumbles, clearly frustrated.

'Well, it does just about everything else,' says Amy. 'I wouldn't get too upset.'

The Doctor's shaking the screwdriver, frowning. 'You just can't rely on modern technology these days!'

The Macra have now surrounded you – their waving pincer-arms form a barricade preventing escape.

'This doesn't look good,' you say.

And you're right. The Macra are herding you away from the beach – towards the entrance of a cave set in the cliff wall. They seem to be moving with one mind. None of them makes any effort to harm you, but it's clear the direction they want you to go in.

You step inside the chilly cave and the Macra urge you on.

'Well, they don't seem to mean us any harm...' notes the Doctor.

'Yet,' says Amy.

'We don't know what they want with us yet,' you say.

'So let's find out,' the Doctor replies.

The Macra herd you down the tunnel into a cavern where flames burn at one end. A circle of Macra surrounds the fire – and Amy grips your arm fearfully.

'I have a really bad feeling about this...'

Go to 10.

The giant crab whirls around, fixing the Doctor with a terrifying stare.

But the Doctor doesn't flinch. 'Can I help you?'

'We are Macra!' the alien declares in a horrible voice.

'Yes, I know what you are — and you're a long way from home. I hope you haven't got any ideas about colonising Earth, because you can forget it. I'm here and you won't get past me.'

The Macra's eyestalks quiver. 'You?'

'Me and my friends, actually.' The Doctor uses his sonic screwdriver to cancel the perception filter, and you, Amy, Mr Jones and all the kids from the school trip reappear.

The Macra looks surprised — but not worried. 'Pleased to meet you,' it gurgles.

'What are the Macra?' someone shouts out. It seems friendly — but it doesn't look it!

'Aliens from the far side of this galaxy,' he explains. 'They live on gas extracts that are completely toxic to human beings. They travel from planet to planet, converting atmospheres for their own use.'

'But that is not why I am here,' says the Macra. Its mandibles clack busily as it speaks. 'We have come to Earth to help. Your climate is spiralling out of control, your continued use of fossil fuels is in jeopardy. The Macra need the fumes your species find so poisonous — we can help each other!'

'I'm not sure,' muses the Doctor. 'We need to think carefully about this...'

If you think the Macra mean well and should be allowed to continue, go to 36.

If you don't think the Macra are here to help, go to 79.

'This way!' you shout, dragging the Doctor and Amy after you.

'Who put you in charge?' asks the Doctor.

'No one,' you reply. 'But sometimes you just have to make a decision – any decision.'

'Decide your own destiny, eh?' the Doctor nods approvingly. 'I like you more and more all the time!'

'Wait a minute,' warns Amy. 'What's that flickering light all about?'

Up ahead is the dim, flickering orange light.

'Flames?' you wonder.

'Something burning,' agrees the Doctor. 'You can feel the heat. Let's take a look!'

The tunnel opens out into a larger cave. The walls are dripping with condensation. On the far side is a low opening full of fire – and grouped around it in a perfect semicircle are six huge Macra!

The flames cast an eerie glow on their red shells and glisten on their eyestalks. Their huge, sharp claws cast great shadows on the walls of the cave.

'What are they doing?' whispers Amy.

The Doctor's eyes are alight with interest. 'It looks like some sort of ceremony!'

If you want to wait where you are and see what happens, go to 19.

If you want to try and get a closer look, creep over to 10.

'Let's ask the Macra.'

The Doctor kneels down before the fallen Macra. Its eyestalks quiver as it tries to focus on the Doctor.

He peers into the alien eyes from beneath his fringe. Neither mind flinches before the other.

'I know you can hear me,' says the Doctor quietly. But there is no mistaking the strength behind those hushed tones. 'I want to help, but first you have to help us. What are you doing here? What do you hope to achieve?'

'We come in peace,' whispers the Macra. Its mouth opens and closes with a horrid sucking noise. 'Humans have tried to change us but there is no need. We wish only to help. We can breathe the gas you humans find so poisonous. We can act as natural processors, rendering it harmless to your species.'

'Well, I'm not exactly human,' the Doctor says, 'but we'll let that go for now. What you describe sounds very interesting – but can we believe you? How do we know you're telling the truth?'

'You cannot,' replies the Macra breathlessly. 'But I give you my word.'

The word of a giant crab? Can you believe it? Should you?

The Doctor's biting his bottom lip. He's thinking about it.

If you want to believe the Macra, go to 36.

If you don't think the Macra is telling the truth, go to 79.

The Doctor and Amy spring into action. The Doctor grabs Rank, quick as a flash, spinning him around. Amy pushes him into the cell, where he lands face down with a big splash.

You're already running before the Doctor shouts, 'Run!'

The other guards can't bring their guns to bear in the narrow passage. The Doctor, Amy and you weave through the soldiers, and they don't know who to aim at first. In another moment you've jumped into the lift and the Doctor's closed the doors.

Alarms start ringing. The Doctor points his sonic screwdriver at the lift controls. 'Going up!'

'Where will this take us?' asks Amy.

The lift shoots up the shaft and gives a cheerful ping as it reaches its destination. The doors slide open and you tumble out into – the reception foyer!

'Back where all this started,' you realise. The police box is still standing in one corner.

'Everyone listen to me!' bellows the Doctor. All the people in the reception area have turned to look. 'Clear the area! It's dangerous to stay in the refinery – this is an emergency! Clear the area!'

After a moment's confusion, everyone starts heading for the exits.

There's a smile on the Doctor's face now – which quickly fades when he hears a terrible banging on the interior doors.

'They're after us,' you realise.

'They'll be through any second...' says Amy.

If you want to make a run for it again, sprint for the exit on 67.

If you want to stand your ground now, go to 22.

'We can ask our friend here some questions,' the Doctor says. He squats down in front of the dying Macra. 'If you answer my questions, I'll switch off the oxygen.'

The Macra waves its eyestalks weakly.

'I'll take that was a yes,' the Doctor smiles. 'OK, here's your starter for ten: what are you doing here on Earth?

The Macra speaks with a low, gurgling voice. 'We are trying to help you humans...'

'I find that hard to believe. And anyway, I'm not human. But go on.'

The Macra coughs. 'We need the gases your planet produces to sustain its energy. Without it we will die! We come in peace...'

'Really?' you ask. 'Then why were you about to operate on me?'

'To see if there is any way we can replicate your respiratory system...'

'So that you're not so reliant on rare toxic gases?' the Doctor says, stroking his chin thoughtfully.

'Surely you don't believe this thing?' asks Amy.

If you think the Macra wants to help mankind, go to 14.

If you think the Macra is lying, go to 79.

You feel rooted to the spot. Every nerve in your body is screaming at you to run – but somehow you can't. Somehow you know you want to see what this thing in the dark really is.

And then a light comes on.

And you wish you hadn't seen it.

Towering above you is the biggest crab you've ever seen – the biggest crab you will probably ever see. Its mouth is poised to bite off your head; thick, gooey saliva hangs from the puckering orifice and it drips on to your shoulders. You can smell the awful breath of the fearsome creature – the nauseous gas that you sensed when you first entered the chamber.

'You've just met the Macra,' says a voice from behind you. 'Say hello.'

You turn to see a man staring up at the Macra – he has a mop of long, untidy hair hanging in a heavy fringe over deep, clever-looking eyes. He's wearing a bow tie and a tweed jacket. And standing beside him is a pretty red-headed girl in a short skirt. She waves at you.

'I'm the Doctor, by the way,' says the man casually. 'And this is Amy. That's all the introductions out of the way. You can tell us your name after I've done this!'

And he points a slim, mechanical device at the giant crab. The air is filled with a shrill noise and the crab – the Macra – backs away, snarling and hissing like an irritated crocodile.

'Sonic screwdriver,' explains the Doctor. 'Works wonders every time. Now come on!'

Amy grabs you by the hand and the three of you race out of the chamber...

... all the way to 8.

The noises are too intriguing. Opening the door, you walk into a vast hangar-like space dominated by huge metal tanks. Pipes and gantries surround the steel cylinders, towering over you.

Something is moving in the shadows at the rear of the chamber.

'Hello?' you call out. 'Anyone there?'

Your voice echoes hollowly and suddenly you feel very alone and vulnerable.

Clang! The door shuts behind you. You're locked in — but with who? Or what?

And then you see.

It creeps slowly out of the gloom — six long, jointed legs supporting a hard carapace surmounted by a pair of blazing eyes on stalks. Huge, crab-like pincers snap at the air in front of you.

The monster advances and you shrink back as its fetid, aquatic breath begins to overwhelm you...

Quick — you'd better get to 65!

'Run for it – again!' roars the Doctor.

You follow him out through the exit. He moves very quickly, with a curious, wild motion – like you never know which direction he's about to take.

You and Amy follow him as best you can through the refinery until you reach a broad expanse of grassland. 'This way!' the Doctor shouts back. 'We need to put some distance between us and the refinery, I think!'

You follow her and the Doctor down a steep slope. Beyond the next rise, the ground turns sandy and before you know it you're running through shallow sand dunes and reedy grass. Behind you, the refinery rises high into the sky – a steel castle of pipes and tubes and scaffolding.

The Doctor and Amy are running along a beach now, kicking up loose sand. They're heading for the waves crashing in on the shore.

With a grin, you follow them down. What's the Doctor planning? A quick paddle? You never know with him!

Find out on 26.

'We could try talking to it,' suggests the Doctor. He creeps cautiously towards the Macra. 'Hello! Do you come here often?'

The Macra's mandibles clack angrily in its mouth.

'I don't think it's working, Doctor,' warns Amy. 'It's going to attack!'

'Look,' you say, moving forward. The light from the Doctor's torch has found a section of controls set in the tunnel wall.

Examining it carefully, the Doctor laughs softly. 'Just what we need – these are emergency access controls for the gas flow to the rest of the refinery.'

'The Macra rely on the gas to breathe,' realises Amy. 'Cut the flow and they're in trouble.'

'Exactly!' The Doctor takes out his sonic screwdriver and sets to work. The Macra growls from the other end of the tunnel, as if sensing the danger.

'You'll have to work quickly,' you say. 'I think he knows what you're up to!'

'This won't take a second,' the Doctor says, operating the controls at lightning speed.

The Macra lurches forward with a terrible roar and you fall back in terror – only to see the giant creature collapse with a mighty clang on the tunnel floor. Its legs scrabble weakly at the metal and its pincers open and close spasmodically. A horrible gasping, sucking noise emanates from its mouth.

'Doctor, it's working!' says Amy. 'The Macra can't breathe!'

'I know,' the Doctor nods sadly. 'That will be happening all over the refinery soon. All the Macra will suffocate.'

'Isn't there anything else you can do?' you ask.

The Doctor's face looks pained, his deep-set eyes full of anguish. 'There's no other choice. If we allow the Macra to continue, they will take over the refinery, pollute the atmosphere of the entire planet and take over. I've seen it before – they are the Scourge of the Galaxy and they never give up.'

The Macra gives a final croak and lies still.

The Doctor locks the gas controls and straightens up. 'That's it – the end of the Macra.'

Silently, Amy follows him out of the tunnel. You join them in the fresh air.

'What happens now?'

The Doctor points in one direction. 'That way the TARDIS.' He points in another direction. 'That way your school party. It's up to you.'

Well – which would you choose...?

THE END

You all make a dash for the caves. The Macra roars and crawls after you, but the three of you are quick enough to reach the cliffs.

'In here!' The Doctor darts into one of the narrow cave entrances. You and Amy both follow him – and not a moment too soon, as the Macra arrives and starts tearing at the rocks behind you with its powerful claws.

But it can't get through the gap.

'Go deeper!' Amy urges.

You press on into the dark of the cave. And then you see a light – flickering a curious blue colour.

'What's that?'

The Doctor's licking his lips with interest. 'Some sort of doorway – I wonder where it leads?'

Find out on 20.

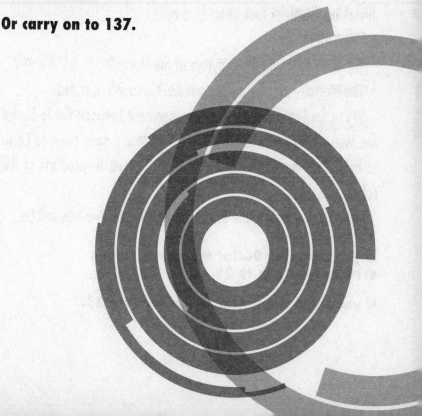

'TARDIS?' you ask, gazing at the police box.

'Time And Relative Dimension In Space,' the Doctor says proudly. 'It can go anywhere and anywhen.'

To be truthful, it doesn't look like much. 'Must be a bit cramped in there,' you say.

'You'd be surprised...' The Doctor opens the door of the TARDIS and ushers you inside.

Click on box C on screen and enter code word TARDIS to see inside.

Or carry on to 137.

'Just a minute, sir,' says a young UNIT trooper. He glares at Professor Greif. 'This man is lying. He used to work for UNIT – but he defected to GasTech and started to experiment on the Macra. He's a traitor to the human race!'

Two more troopers move in and arrest the professor, binding his wrists with plasticuffs. He tries to protest but he's led away to a UNIT troop carrier.

'What about us?' asks Amy.

'You're under arrest as well,' the UNIT soldier says. There's no mistaking the bleak look in his blue eyes.

'What for?'

'Trying to sabotage the activities of the Macra.'

'The Macra – aren't they the baddies?' you ask, puzzled.

'We're facilitating a business arrangement between GasTech and the Macra,' explains the UNIT man. 'The Macra have come to Earth to help. They have agreed to consume the toxic by-products of the refinery in exchange for sanctuary.'

Instantly you look to the Doctor to see what his reaction will be...

If you think the Doctor will agree to this arrangement, go to 28.

If you think the Doctor will object, try 33.

You push the door open, and it leads into another corridor. There is a different smell here — something industrial, like the exhaust fumes of a car.

This corridor isn't as bright and clinical as the first. In fact it's pretty dark, because the lights aren't working properly.

'Hang on a mo,' says a voice from the shadows. 'I'll fix the lights.'

There's a shrill whine and suddenly the whole corridor is illuminated by powerful strip lighting.

Standing in the middle of the passage is a man in a tweedy jacket and elbow patches. He's sporting a bow tie and narrow trousers and looks like he might be a teacher or a professor, except he's so young. Bright eyes turn to look at you from beneath a heavy black fringe.

'Oh dear,' he says, his shoulders slumping. 'We've got company.'

A red-headed girl in a short skirt steps out from behind him. 'Are you lost?' she asks you with a smile.

'No,' you reply. 'Are you?'

'More often that not,' says the man. 'But, if I'm honest, I prefer it that way. Makes life so much more interesting, don't you think?'

You nod in agreement, warming to him straight away. He's not smiling, but there's a twinkle in those deep-set eyes all the same.

'How did you get the lights to work?' you ask.

'Ah! Inquisitive, good, like that.' He holds up a slim metal device. 'Sonic screwdriver, multi-purpose, multi-function, multi-multi. Like it?'

You nod again.

'Great! We're going to get on really well.' The man holds out his hand. 'I'm the Doctor and this is Amy.'

You tell him your name but he's already withdrawn his hand and is peering back down the corridor. 'Can you smell something?' the Doctor asks.

'It's not me, honest,' says the girl, Amy.

'Or me!' you add quickly.

The Doctor's sniffing loudly like a dog with a scent. 'Definitely not me either. Well, that's a relief. Could be embarrassing otherwise. But on the other hand...'

He sniffs again.

'Don't mind him,' advises Amy with a smile. 'He's always like this.'

'Wait!' exclaims the Doctor suddenly, holding up a hand. 'Can you hear that? Listen!'

You all strain to hear — a strange, distant hissing noise echoing along the corridor.

'Still not me,' says Amy.

'Or me!' you say at the same time as the Doctor.

The Doctor runs down to the end of the corridor and is calling you to follow. The passageway branches off in two directions.

'The noise came from down there,' the Doctor says, pointing one way.

'The smell's coming from the other direction, though,' says Amy, wafting a hand in front of her nose. 'Yuck.'

If you want to investigate the strange noise, follow the corridor to 100.

If you want to follow the strange smell, try 110.

Cautiously you open the door. The Doctor leads the creature slowly out. It's terrified, literally shaking, but it seems to trust him. It's very easy to trust the Doctor.

The guards outside instinctively fall back. They're not sure what to do — but they can see the Macra-man is something extraordinary. They grip their weapons nervously, waiting for orders from their captain.

'What the heck is that?' the guard captain asks.

The Macra-man twitches anxiously and the Doctor holds a finger to his lips. 'Shh. My friend here is very, very frightened of you. And who can blame him? He might look like a crab but you're the ones with the guns.'

But one of the guards has the creature in his sights, and he's very nervous. His fingers are tight on the machine gun, the knuckles white. He licks his lips.

'Lower your weapon,' orders the Doctor.

The Macra-man has sensed the danger, however, and a low, gurgling noise comes from its throat. The mandibles open wide, hissing at the soldier.

His nerve breaks and he opens fire.

'No!' screams the Doctor over the deafening rattle of the gun.

The crab-man's shell splinters as the fusillade of bullets strike, spinning him around and out of the Doctor's arms.

The Doctor is outraged, turning furiously on the guards with blazing anger in his eyes. But they're armed and blood is in the air. You and Amy both grab the Doctor and drag him away...

Take him to 132.

'We should get away from here,' Amy says. 'There's no way of knowing what's going on in there. Could be poison gas – anything.'

The Doctor pulls a face. 'If it's poison gas then the Macra should be happy. They like that kind of thing.'

'But we should still get away while we still can,' Amy insists. 'Let's get back to the Control Tower and inform the authorities.'

The Doctor agrees and the three of you leave by the exterior exit door. The fresh air lifts your spirits slightly and clears your head. You've survived an encounter with a hostile alien creature! The Doctor and Amy seem to have taken this in their stride, like they do it all the time.

'We need to get our friend here back to that school trip,' Amy says.

The Doctor nods again. 'Oh, yeah, right. School trip. Ho hum. Macra – interesting!'

That's more like it! You grin and the Doctor grins back. Then he takes a sudden left-hand turn, ducking under a series of huge gas pipes, and scampering off in an apparently random direction.

'Where are we going?' you ask, hurrying after him with Amy.

'I can smell the beach!'

You reach the outer perimeter of the refinery. Through a chain-mesh fence you can see grassland sloping down to a cliff edge and the coast. The Doctor was right!

Head for the beach on 67.

The Macra lets out a blood-curdling shriek. Its claws snap madly at nothing as the ultrasonic vibrations penetrate deep into its shell – right down to the soft tissues beneath.

And then, with a sudden, loud *squelch*! the Macra seems to burst open. Its shell splits apart at the seams and a thick, sinuous slime erupts from the gap. With a final shudder, the monster collapses, dead.

'That signal is being broadcast right around the refinery,' announces the Doctor grimly. He speaks softly, but firmly.

You are all aware of exactly what it means. He takes no pleasure from it, nor any satisfaction. But the Doctor would not let an alien menace like that destroy the human race.

All over the gas refinery, the amplified ultrasonic signal forces the Macra into a state of collapse, cracking open their shells and liquidising their innards.

Eventually, silently, the Doctor closes down the public address system and switches off the sonic screwdriver.

Everyone is quiet. There is no cheering or jubilation. Everyone understands what has happened. The Macra are all finished.

'They should never have come here,' the Doctor says quietly. And then he stands up and tells the scientists that they must take control of the refinery and close it down and alert the authorities to the dangers of GasTech.

'And what will you do?' the chief scientist asks.

'Go,' replies the Doctor simply. 'But not before we make sure our friend here gets back to his school party.'

You realise he means you – what a long time ago it seems since the start of your school trip!

THE END

Minutes later, you're trudging along the beach in the shadow of the refinery.

The Doctor seems in good spirits – damp and bedraggled, but still optimistic. 'We have to tackle this problem at source. The Macra have to be stopped – if they take control of the refinery it will be goodbye Earth!'

Further along the shore, Amy spots tracks in the gritty sand.

'Macra tracks,' says the Doctor, examining the deep grooves left by many claw-like legs. 'You can see how they move sideways like a normal Earth crab. Except they're not normal. And there are many different kinds of Macra – some big, intelligent and mean. Others are huge, savage and bloodthirsty. Then there are some which have reached a high enough state of intelligence to reason with them.'

'Let's hope these are the tracks of the last lot, then,' you say.

Find out on 122.

'I know where they'll be,' you tell Amy. 'Heading back to the reception area, probably.'

'The Control Tower?' queries the Doctor. 'Be careful — there's something very odd going on here.'

You hurry off with Amy, winding your way through the labyrinth of pipes and tubes — until you hear voices ahead. It's the school trip. The teacher in charge, Mr Jones, seems to be lost.

'I knew we should never have come this way!' he grumbles.

You step into view with Amy.

'Mr Jones — it's not safe here,' you say. 'You'd best come with us.'

He looks disgruntled but also slightly relieved. 'You seem to be leading us on a wild goose chase! Who's your friend?'

'I'm Amy Pond,' she says, with a bright, welcoming smile. But she's also firm: 'Follow us, please, and don't lag behind.'

She turns before Mr Jones has a chance to argue — and heads back towards the Doctor. The school party, chattering excitedly, fall in behind her.

'Where are we going?' asks Mr Jones.

But there's no time for proper explanations. Very soon, you're all back with the Doctor. He's found a large entrance door to one of the biggest silos in the refinery. There are gasps of awe from the kids, and a lot of excited questions, but he waves them to silence.

'Is there any point to all this?' Mr Jones asks crossly.

The Doctor just smiles and shrugs. 'Let's find out, shall we?'

He uses the sonic screwdriver to unlock the door, and then leads the way inside. You all follow. The school kids have fallen completely silent, overawed by the experience.

Inside the silo is a strange chamber, lit green, with the walls covered in some kind of hard, undulating substance. Lights flash in random order on what appear to be control banks of some kind.

'What is it?' wonders Amy, feeling the walls.

'Chitin,' replies the Doctor thoughtfully. 'Shell. Organic, but as hard as rock. Grown rather than manufactured. It's all very odd.'

'And are these some kind of controls?' you ask, indicating a bank of strange lights growing out of the floor. The school party gathers around, craning their necks to see, as the Doctor examines the object.

'It's not just any control panel,' he says. 'These are the kind of controls I'd expect to find on a sophisticated teleport system.'

'This is all alien, isn't it?' realises Amy, looking around.

The Doctor nods. 'Yes — and I've got a shrewd idea what kind of alien. But it doesn't make sense. Unless...'

Suddenly the teleport controls start to flash and hum. The chamber fills with a sizzling electric energy field, and everyone backs away.

'Hang on,' says the Doctor. 'The teleport is operating - something's coming through!'

If you think you should try to stop the teleport, go to 35.

If you'd think everyone would be better off hiding, go to 94.

You're about to explore a little further when you hear voices — a man and a woman.

You peek around the corner of the silo and see two people. The first is a striking redhead in a short skirt. The other is a man in a tweedy jacket and bow tie. Oddly, his trousers look a little too short and he's wearing boots. They are chatting enthusiastically about something in the man's hand — a slim metallic device with a glowing green tip.

'But, Doctor,' says the girl, 'We've been here hours and we've not found any sign of alien activity.'

'The sonic screwdriver's never wrong, Amy,' replies the Doctor. He shakes the device and listens to it carefully. 'Unless it's still got frost in it from that last trip to Antarctica...'

'Hello...' Amy says, spotting you. 'Looks like we've got company, Doctor.'

The Doctor scans you with the screwdriver. 'Well, that's no alien.'

'Are you really looking for aliens here?' you ask.

Amy jerks a thumb at the Doctor. 'The Doctor here thinks there's something odd going on at the refinery.'

'The TARDIS did pick up some very peculiar energy readings as we came in to land,' the Doctor nods. 'And there is a gas signature here which makes me think of Macra.'

'Macra?' you repeat.

'Giant alien crab monsters.' Amy just looks at you and shrugs.

'We had to investigate, Amy,' insists the Doctor. 'It'd be rude not to.'

'So what now?' Amy asks.

The Doctor shrugs. 'Back into the refinery, have another look around.'

If you smell something strange and want to investigate, go to 92.

If you want to go straight back indoors, head for 18.

'You must think I was born yesterday,' says the Doctor. 'The Macra are always looking for worlds to invade and corrupt. They're an infestation – once they get a grip on a planet, it's very difficult to get rid of them!'

The Macra hisses angrily. 'You know our species!'

'Yeah – so clear off.'

'We have already secured a bridgehead on this planet – we control this refinery!'

'No, you don't.' The Doctor produces his sonic screwdriver and aims it at the control banks of the Macra's teleportation device. 'I do.'

'Explain!'

'I thought it was you lot by the smell when I got here. So I've set the controls to a reverse teleport signal – all I have to do is activate it.' The Doctor waggles the screwdriver. 'If I'm not mistaken, the teleport's tuned into Macra life-forms, so it will affect you all.'

The Macra snaps its claws angrily. 'You would not dare! Reversing the teleport signal would kill us all!'

'Possibly. But there are other options.' The Doctor turns to look at you. 'What do you think?'

If you think the Doctor should find another way to deal with the Macra, go to 31.

If you think he should press home his advantage now, go to 116.

You help Amy haul the Doctor's inert body towards the door. The Macra is still trying to force its way through the narrow gap. The shell is scraping loudly against the edge of the concrete.

Together you drag the Doctor's body across the floor. He's muttering to himself, still half-unconscious.

The Macra thrashes and roars, insane with hunger.

You kick the door open, just as Amy is grabbed by the Macra! It's caught the edge of her top with its pincer. You grab her hand and wrench her backwards. The material of her top tears and all the Macra has for its effort is a fragment of cloth.

Amy stumbles through the door and you push the Doctor out after her.

Slam! You close the door on the bellowing monster. The whole wall seems to be shaking. You can still hear it smashing around inside.

'Well, that was worse than useless!' Amy says, wrinkling her nose at the sonic screwdriver.

'Don't diss the sonic screwdriver!' warns the Doctor, snatching the screwdriver. He's sat up, his hair tousled but his eyes bright – fully awake again! 'Right – Macra, knock on the head, escape. Well done, both of you. But there's one thing you've overlooked.'

You exchange a glance with Amy and shrug. 'What?'

'Listen.'

You can't hear anything.

'Exactly,' nods the Doctor. 'The Macra's stopped. No roaring, no crashing around like a mad thing.'

And he's right – there's complete silence from the next room.

'Wonder what's going on in there?' says the Doctor.

If you want to find out why it's gone quiet, go to 130.

If you would rather get away while you can, go to 74.

'Keep going!'

The Doctor leads the way, holding his flickering match up to light the way as best he can. It's barely adequate. Amy follows, and you bring up the rear. All you can see in front of you is the dim orange glow of the match light against the narrowing rock walls. All you can hear behind you is the clatter of the Macra giving chase.

But eventually, the tunnel does widen out — and the three of you collapse to your knees with exhaustion. You're sweating and covered with grime and your clothes are torn and filthy.

But the Doctor seems to revel in it!

He's up on his feet again, holding the match out in front of him — you can't begin to guess how it's lasted so long!

'Who's for a nice swim?' he asks enthusiastically.

There's a large pool of water stretching out into the darkness. The Doctor hurls a stone into the middle and it disappears with a loud *plop!* It sounds quite deep.

'You've got to be kidding,' says Amy.

'There's no way back, unless you fancy being breakfast for the Macra horde,' the Doctor says. 'And the only way forward is through that.' He points at the pool.

You can already hear the Macra scrabbling through the rock fissure behind you. There isn't much time.

'No need to get your costume,' the Doctor continues breezily. And then he leaps into the pool with an enormous splash. 'Come on in, the water's lovely!' he shouts as he reappears.

It's not. It's brutally cold and very murky.

'How far do we have to swim?' asks Amy, her teeth chattering.

'As far as it takes,' replies the Doctor. And then he sets off with a powerful front crawl.

You take a deep breath and follow...

Swim all the way to 126.

You take the right hand passage, following the Doctor. It's very dark, and his voice echoes back from the shadows:

'This is part of the refinery pipe line, it could go on for miles.'

'I hope that smell doesn't go on for miles,' says Amy. She's holding a handkerchief over her mouth and nose.

'Fresh air up ahead!' announces the Doctor.

You reach a hatchway at the end of the pipeline. There's a grille set in the door and you can feel a breeze blowing gently through it, bearing the unmistakable scent of freedom.

Quickly the Doctor sonics the latch on the door and kicks it open. You all pile out into a bright, sunny afternoon. Blinking, eyes watering, you try to get your bearings.

'Where on Earth are we now?' wonders Amy.

'Still on Earth, of course,' replies the Doctor. 'No worries there. As to where exactly – well, let's see what's over this way...'

You follow the Doctor away from the great mass of pipes and ducts rising up around the edge of the gas refinery. There's a salty breeze blowing in from the coast.

'Hope you've brought your bucket and spade!' laughs the Doctor.

Are you all heading for the seaside? Find out on 76.

The steam drifts away to reveal a figure lying inside the casket like a corpse in a coffin.

But this is no human being. The body is covered with segments of hard, red shell rather than skin. The arms end in hooked pincers. The face is a nightmare mixture of human and crab!

The creature's eyes snap open, extending suddenly on stalks from the empty black sockets.

You all rear backwards as the eyes wave around, panic stricken. The crab-man thrashes in the casket, lurching up with a gurgling cry of shock and fear.

'It's all right,' says the Doctor, holding the strange figure firmly by the shoulders. 'It's all right. Shh. I've got you. You're safe.'

The crab-man sobs pathetically, its eyes withdrawing into the shell covering its head. Its mouth puckers open, showing mandibles instead of jaws.

'What is it?' you ask, stunned.

The Doctor rocks the creature gently. 'Some sort of human-Macra amalgam. I don't know whether it's deliberate or accidental, but it isn't natural. It's got to stop.'

There is a dark, serious look in the Doctor's eyes, but the Macra-man seems calmer in his company.

'What can we do?' Amy wonders as the Doctor helps the quivering figure from the casket.

But the banging on the door increases — and you can hear the shouts of the guards outside.

'We're trapped,' you realise. 'There's no other way out.'

'Let them in,' orders the Doctor bleakly.

Open the door to 73.

The Doctor opens the connecting door and walks calmly through, sonic screwdriver at the ready.

'I've set the screwdriver's frequency to one that calms the fear centres of the Macra brain,' he whispers. 'Should help keep things cool.'

The room is full of Macra, and a foul-smelling, swirling gas.

'It's pretty toxic,' the Doctor warns. 'Lovely for the Macra — not so good for us, but we'll be OK for a short while.'

Even so, you and Amy both cover your nose and mouth with handkerchiefs.

Soon, the Doctor establishes contact with the Macra leader, a powerful creature with a thick, gnarled carapace and huge claws. It eyes the Doctor warily.

'Hi,' the Doctor says. 'Glad you're all feeling better. What's the deal here, then?'

'We wish to help Earth with its pollution problem,' replied the giant crab creature. 'We offer the Macra Accord — a business relationship whereby we are allowed to breathe the gas humans find toxic.'

'Very decent of you. There's plenty of room for you here at the refinery if you want to stay and help.'

'Some of us will stay,' rumbles the Macra leader. 'There are many of us here with different skills and needs. Some will volunteer to stay on Earth and help your scientists solve the problems of environmental pollution. Others must return to the stars.'

The Doctor is beaming. 'Excellent!'

'The Macra Accord could not have been made without your help, Doctor. We all owe you — and your friends — a great debt of thanks.'

Amy shares a smile with you, and you realise your adventure is over. It's been quite a day — and some school trip!

THE END

'Shouldn't be any problem getting inside,' the Doctor assures you. He uses the sonic screwdriver to cut a hole in the chain link fence.

'I thought you said it was a screwdriver?' you say, climbing through the hole with Amy.

'It's sonic — and much more besides,' the Doctor says. As you walk towards the refinery, he shows you the device.

If you want a closer look at the sonic screwdriver, click on box D and enter code word SONIC.

Or go to 138.

'I'd like to believe you, really, I would,' sighs the Doctor. 'But I'm afraid that's not going to happen. I know the Macra of old – in the future, and even farther into the future. They never bear any goodwill to mankind. They are a thoroughly nasty lot, and Earth could well do without them.'

Amy looks uncertainly between the Doctor and the Macra. 'Are you sure? He seems so... nice.'

'They can be very clever,' admits the Doctor. 'But not as clever as – *this!*'

Instantly, he whirls into action – leaping across the chamber, splashing through the tank. The Macra reels back in confusion – snapping its claws at the Doctor's coat tails as he flashes by.

The Doctor dives – straight towards a set of heavy levers emerging from the floor. He yanks one down and there's an immediate, devastating whoosh of air – and the water starts to drain from the pool, sucked down like the flush in a toilet!

The Macra groans, its legs scrabbling at the edges of the tank.

'Get out, quick!' roars the Doctor.

You head for the exit, Amy right behind you. Flinging open the doors, you shoot out into the bright daylight.

Go straight to 9.

You're in complete darkness. It's cold. You're sitting close to Amy and the Doctor for warmth. All you can see is the steady pulse of the sonic screwdriver.

You've been like this for ages.

But then you hear the rocks moving!

'Is it the Macra again?' wonders Amy nervously.

'I doubt it!' says the Doctor, helping clear some of the debris. Then a brilliant light shines through and illuminates his face – which breaks into a wide smile.

'It's a rescue!'

A man appears in a helmet with the torch mounted on it. He's wearing overalls and what looks like potholing gear.

'It's mountain rescue!' realises Amy.

'They got my signal!' cries the Doctor, waving the sonic screwdriver delightedly.

There are military personnel there too – dressed in black with red berets, carrying guns and equipment.

It's UNIT – the Unified Intelligence Taskforce and they're pulling you up to safety.

If you want to stay and help UNIT, go to 27.

If you would prefer to leave now, go to 32.

The TARDIS materialises underground. Its wheezing and groaning noise echoes down the length of a subterranean tunnel. You step out of the amazing police box feeling slightly disorientated.

'Don't worry, it's only to be expected,' Amy tells you. 'It can be a bit weird, travelling in the TARDIS.'

The Doctor locks the police box and starts down the tunnel, aiming a flashlight up and down the walls. They are dripping with condensation and it is extremely cold.

'How deep are we?' wonders Amy, shivering.

'Too deep,' responds the Doctor immediately. 'Way too deep. I've missed the substrata gas lines by a good two hundred metres or more. Perhaps those short hops are harder than I thought!'

'There's a way out down here by the looks of it,' you say. There is light up ahead and fresh air.

You emerge in the mouth of a cave overlooking a beach.

'Look!' exclaims the Doctor. 'We're at the seaside!'

You and Amy exchange a puzzled frown. The seaside?

'Geronimo!' yells the Doctor, rushing out on to the sand.

Follow him to 141.

After only a moment's hesitation, you follow the tour party. The refinery is huge and you don't want to get lost.

At least not yet.

In the next room, there's a presentation by the owner of the gas company, Sebastian Quipe. The GasTech refinery, he claims, is the very latest in liquid gas conversion. The energy it produces is clean and economically perfect.

OK, so you're already bored. Most of the kids are as well. But you've noticed something they haven't.

On the other side of the room is a tall blue box with little white-framed windows and a lamp on the roof. A notice above the doors says POLICE BOX. It looks completely out of place.

You're about to wander over for a closer look when someone brushes past you. At first you think it's a teacher — he's young, with a shock of unruly dark hair, and he's wearing a tweed jacket with elbow patches and narrow trousers.

If you want to see what the man does, go straight to 139.

Or you could check out the police box on 42.

'Sounds good,' Amy says.

'Too good to be true,' you mutter. Surely it can't be that simple?

But perhaps it is. The Doctor is already in the middle of another laboratory, eagerly examining the readouts on a number of computer monitors controlled by white-coated scientists. He's in his element, scuttling from one screen to another, making notes, clapping people on the back, flicking his hair out of his eyes as he studies the data.

'This is fascinating,' he says enthusiastically. But then his face falls. 'And wrong.'

'Wrong?' echoes Quipe.

'The Macra don't help other species out — especially not humans. They prefer to take what they want, by force or guile. And what they want is an atmosphere they can breathe. Poisonous to you lot, but great for them.'

'Here we can live in harmony,' Quipe insists.

The Doctor shakes his head. 'Nothing is ever that simple. There has to be a snag. What's all this about Experiment Z?'

'Experiment Z?'

'I saw it referred to on one of the data stations,' the Doctor explains. 'Lots of unusual genetic cross sampling. At a glance I'd say human and Macra.' His expression hardens as he stares at Quipe. 'What's going on here?'

'Show them Experiment Z,' instructs Quipe.

You are taken to a side chamber, where a thick glass window looks on to a sterile white room. The door is hermetically sealed – nothing can get in or out. Lying on a white table in the middle of the room is a human body.

A hatchway opens on the far wall and a Macra is revealed. It crawls forward, pincers snapping. On the end of its stunted secondary arms are a number of gleaming steel blades and surgical instruments. The Macra advances on the human body, its eyes quivering on the end of stalks.

'This is monstrous,' snarls the Doctor angrily.

'This is progress,' says Quipe. 'The Macra are helping us to discover a way for humans to breath in a poisonous atmosphere.'

'I doubt that very much!'

If you think you should contact the authorities, go to 43.

If you think you should leave while you still can, go to 54.

The Doctor points the sonic screwdriver at the nearest Macra. The tip glows a brilliant green and a shrill vibration fills the air.

'It's not working!' says Amy as the Macra continues its inexorable approach.

The Doctor quickly tries another setting. He aims the sonic screwdriver again – still no response.

'It's gaining on us!' you shout.

Another adjustment. He tries again – and this time there's a result! The whine is almost inaudible, it's so high up the sonic range, but the Macra is clearly affected. It shudders and writhes, crawling backwards, its eyes withdrawing on their long stalks.

The Doctor stands up, holding the sonic screwdriver straight out. The Macra retreat even further. He starts swinging it in a low arc, forcing more of the monsters to back off.

'We're lucky,' he says. 'They're still a bit tender after shedding their shells. This would never have worked on a fully mature Macra!'

'You've cleared a path to that tunnel entrance!' you realise, pointing at a dark, circular opening in the cliff wall behind you. 'They won't be able to follow us in there if we get through the grille.'

Backing away from the Macra, keeping the screwdriver trained on the more daring specimens, the three of you reach the shaft entrance. Amy and you unlatch the grille and then refasten it behind you.

The Doctor switches off the sonic screwdriver and starts down the tunnel. 'Come on – this way!'

You haven't gone far before a low, rumbling growl echoes down the tunnel. The Doctor holds up a hand to stop you. 'Uh-oh...'

'What is it?' you ask.

'Giant Macra, right at the end of the tunnel!'

'What now?'

Find out on 68.

'Definitely smelled that smell before...' says the Doctor, following his nose.

You all follow the Doctor's nose. The smell is strange – rotten, putrid, almost choking as it gets stronger and stronger.

'Are you sure this is safe?' asks Amy.

'No. Are you?'

A narrow doorway leads into a wide, brightly-lit workshop. There are benches and heavy tools all around, electric cables snaking across the floor and monitors everywhere.

But by far the strangest thing here is the giant crab spread-eagled on the central bench – a huge beast the size of a small car, resting on its shell, legs held down and away by heavy cables. Enormous claws are held fast by steel clamps attached to the ceiling.

'What is that?'

The Doctor's frowning. 'A Macra,' he replies. 'Alien life form from another solar system. No wonder I could smell the gas...'

'But why is it tied down like that?' asks Amy.

'Are they experimenting on it?' you wonder.

'Or torturing it,' mutters the Doctor darkly.

Ping! You all look across the room to a set of double doors. Above the doors a light has started to flash.

'It's a lift,' Amy realises. 'Someone's coming...!'

If you want to hide before the lift arrives, duck down behind a bench on 102.

If you want to stay and confront whoever it is, stand your ground on 125.

You wake up with a splitting headache. Amy is by your side, helping you to your feet.

'Take it easy, you've had a bad knock on the head.'

There are no Macra around. You're alone with Amy in some kind of waiting room — comfortable chairs, a low table, a drinks machine. She fetches you a glass of water.

'What happened?'

'The Macra went berserk,' Amy explains. 'I managed to drag you and the Doctor out, though. We're in a side lab.'

'Where's the Doctor?'

A door opens and the Doctor crashes in, a whirl of arms and legs and excited energy. 'Come on, you two — no time to sit around looking sorry for yourselves. We've got work to do. Come and look at this!'

He bounds back through the door and you follow him with Amy.

Follow the Doctor to 113.

'Quickly,' orders the Doctor, 'hide!'

You all look around for a hiding place – but it's not easy.

'Doctor! There are about twenty of us in here!' points out Amy.

The teleport is humming loudly now, and a coruscating energy field has materialised in the middle of the chamber.

The Doctor is hopping from control to control, desperately sonicing with his screwdriver. 'I can't stop the teleport operating – the transmission field is already fully committed. We'll have company any second now...'

'There must be something we can do!'

'We'll hide!' the Doctor insists, working feverishly at one of the strange consoles as the teleport reaches a crescendo. If I can just create some kind of perception filter...'

He finishes working with a flourish, and everyone disappears!

'What's happened?' you exclaim – you can see yourself, but no one else. Where have they all gone?

'We're all invisible to each other,' explains the Doctor quickly. 'And, hopefully, to whoever's coming through the teleport! Now, shhh!'

The teleport field fades and in its place stands a terrifying creature – a giant crab, with enormous claws and glossy black eyes protruding from stalks. It scuttles across the chamber and makes careful adjustments to the control consoles with surprisingly delicate use of its smaller, jointed forearms.

Suddenly, the Doctor appears – seemingly out of thin air as he adjusts the perception filter.

'Hello!' he announces cheerfully, tapping the giant crab on its shell. 'Can I have a word?'

Go to 60.

It's like a prison cell. The only source of light is a bare bulb in a recess in the ceiling. It's cold and damp and you start shivering.

'Look,' you shout, pointing at the water. It's starting to slosh about as if disturbed from underneath. 'What's that all about?'

The Doctor and Amy move closer to the foaming water. Suddenly a seething mass of legs and claws erupts from the depths as hundreds of crabs scramble up the slope, surging towards you.

'Incredible!' gasps the Doctor. 'Something I thought I'd never see!'

'What? Crabs?'

'Not just crabs – infant Macra!' The Doctor claps his hands, eyes gleaming with excitement. 'Crustaceous alien life form from another galaxy,' he explains. 'They can come in many forms – but seeing them in their infant state is very rare!'

You eye the Macra suspiciously as they crawl out of the water. There must be hundreds of them, snipping and snapping with their little claws. They look terrifying. 'Are they dangerous?'

'Very!'

Amy yelps as a Macra snaps at her feet. She scurries back towards the door and the Doctor hurriedly sonics the lock.

'Hurry!' you yell.

'Ten more seconds!' yells the Doctor.

'There'll be on us in five!'

The crabs advance up the slope in a wild, clattering horde...

Quick - back away to 57.

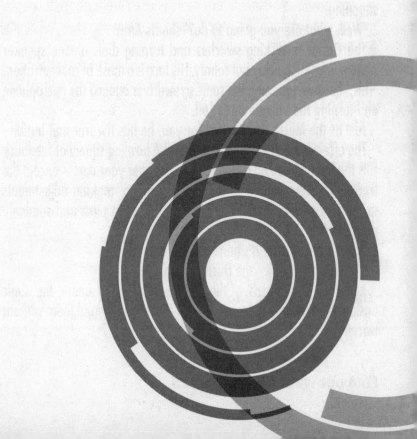

Amy looks anxiously at the Doctor. 'Have we really got time to make a public announcement?' she asks, as the Macra forces its way through the doors.

'We can't just leave everyone to die!' protests the scientist.

'I'm not going to make a public service announcement,' snaps the Doctor, sitting down at the public address system. 'Do I look like the BBC?'

The Macra forces the door fully open and begins to scrabble through the entrance, its claw-like legs ripping aside the workbench and scattering equipment. With a hiss of anger it enters the lab, claws snapping.

'Well, what are you going to do?' shouts Amy.

The Doctor is flicking switches and turning dials on the speaker system, moving quickly but calmly. His face is a mask of concentration. 'This,' he says, jamming the sonic screwdriver against the microphone and turning the volume up to full.

Just as the Macra reaches out for you, he hits the transmit button.

The effect is electric – and deafening! A howling squeal of feedback fills the lab and you all clamp your hands over your ears – except the Doctor. He stays rooted to the spot, frowning, making adjustments to the screwdriver as the terrible shriek rises in pitch and suddenly disappears.

'What's happened? It's gone quiet!'

'I'm into ultrasonic,' the Doctor declares.

And then it happens – the Macra, shuddering under the sonic onslaught, suddenly rears up. Its legs thrash madly and then, without warning...

Find out what happens on 75.

You wake up looking at the ceiling. Bright lights. A harsh, antiseptic smell. You're lying on a table of some kind — it could be an operating table. You're tied down — straps across your wrists and ankles and forehead. You can't see anything else except the lights above.

And then a shadow passes over you.

A pair of wicked black eyes stare down at you from the end of long, flexible stalks. A wet mouth puckers inside a narrow gap between hard red shell.

The Macra lets out a sigh of satisfaction, its rank breath washing over you. A pair of huge pincers fills your vision as it leans over you.

Your heart is pounding with fear — but out of the corner of your eye you can see two figures sneaking into the operating room. It's the Doctor and Amy!

Thank goodness they're still alive and free!

If you think you'd better cause a distraction so they are not noticed, go to 23.

If you think they should get out while they still can, shout a warning on 58.

'Hold on,' whispers the Doctor. 'I want to stay and watch for a while...'
But the Macra that have shed their old shells are starting to explore
the area around the rock pools. Their new shells are beginning to
form – turning stiff and opaque under the light of the sun.

'Some of those things are getting a bit close,' warns Amy.

'But this is amazing!' the Doctor protests. 'We could be one of the
very few humanoid life forms ever to have witnessed this process!'

'And we don't want to be one of the very last, either,' Amy replies.

'Look out!' you cry. One of the Macra has crept much closer than
expected – silently creeping over the sand towards your hiding
position. Its shell is almost fully formed and its pincers look deadly.
Its twin black eyes are fixed on you.

And there are others approaching – it's almost as if they have sensed
the interest of the first and now they are all aware of your presence.
With an excited hissing and chattering, they start to converge on the
three of you.

'Oops,' mutters the Doctor helpfully.

'Time for a great idea, Doctor...'

He fishes in his pocket and produces the trusty sonic screwdriver.

'Does it have an anti-Macra setting?' you ask.

He grins. 'Time to find out!'

**If you think the sonic screwdriver will work,
go to 91.**

**If you don't think it will have any effect,
go to 59.**

'My first priority is Amy,' the Doctor tells you firmly. There's a look in those deep-set eyes that chills you to the bone.

He leads you into another part of the refinery, where several huge tanks of liquid gas dominate a room the size of an aircraft hangar.

'What makes you think Amy came this way?' you ask.

'She was looking for signs of alien life,' the Doctor replies simply, searching along the maze of pipes connecting the gas tanks to the refinery.

'Alien life?'

'Ugly, hard, brutal, and probably breathing toxic fumes,' the Doctor nods. 'This place – perfect breeding ground.' He stops to rest his ear against one of the tanks. 'Listen to that!'

You press your ear to the cold metal. You can't hear much, except for the rhythmic pump of the refinery machine. 'Some kind of pump?'

'Yes,' the Doctor agrees. 'But not the kind you're thinking of. It's not mechanical – it's biological. Alive.'

You suddenly realise what he means. 'It's a heartbeat!'

The Doctor opens the access door to the tank with his sonic screwdriver. Inside it's pitch black. 'Well – do you want to go first, or shall I?'

If you want to go in first, go to 120.

If you would rather follow the Doctor, go to 29.

The passageway leads to a heavy door, locked and bolted. The Doctor opens it with his sonic screwdriver and the three of you emerge into the cold afternoon air.

'We're outside,' you realise.

'Right in the heart of the operation,' Amy nods.

You are surrounded by a complex network of pipes and tanks. Steam drifts past from a number of valves set into a series of thick tubes leading directly into the ground.

'Sound is louder this way,' announces the Doctor, moving to a large, cylindrical storage tank. It rises above you, blocking out the sky. The Doctor circles it, listening intently.

'What are you looking for?' you ask Amy.

'You wouldn't believe me if I told you,' she replies.

Before you can ask any more questions, the Doctor calls you both over. He's found a door into the silo and it's open.

'Follow me,' he says, 'but watch your step.'

The three of you climb into the silo. It's empty – but dark and claustrophobic. The Doctor uses a pencil torch to light the way, examining the inside of the tank.

'Just bare metal walls,' you remark.

'But what's that smell?' The Doctor is pacing up and down, sniffing. 'What is it?'

Clang! The door shuts behind you and bolts slam home. You don't need to try it to know that it's locked.

'We're trapped,' realises Amy anxiously.

'That smell's getting worse, you know,' remarks the Doctor, apparently unconcerned. 'It's like some kind of...' Suddenly he whirls around, consternation all over his face. 'Gas! It's poisonous gas!'

You're already coughing. The smell is foul and you can barely breathe – Amy's the same. The gas is flooding into the sealed chamber. You can see wisps of it floating from the end of a pipe in the wall.

'Do something!' splutters Amy, covering her face with a handkerchief.

'Quick!' the Doctor orders. 'Help me!'

If you want to try blocking the pipe, go to 2.

If you think you should try to open the hatch and escape, go to 53.

Amy points the sonic screwdriver at the Macra and activates it. A shrill whine fills the chamber, almost drowning out the snarls of the giant crab. Green light flickers from the screwdriver's tip — but will it work?

The Macra thrashes from side to side, its legs skittering on the concrete floor. The huge pincers snap wildly, and a terrible roar echoes around the room. Saliva from the flapping mandibles sprays through the air.

'You've made it angry!' you realise.

The Macra surges forward with a bestial snarl. You help Amy pull the unconscious Doctor towards the door. The Macra is almost too big for the room — it splashes out of its tank but the hard shell gets wedged in the steel girders which line the ceiling. It hisses with fury, stretching out its claws and snapping at your heels.

'Get out!' Amy cries, pushing you towards the door. 'There are controls outside — you can activate the force field!'

But she can't pull the Doctor out by herself. If you stay, you run the risk of being killed by the Macra. If you go, you'll be leaving Amy and the Doctor to an uncertain fate...

If you want to get out now and try to save them from the outside, head for 9.

If you think you should stay and help, go to 80.

The lift door opens and an elderly man with a beard and white coat shuffles in. He's concentrating on a clipboard and doesn't notice the three of you crouched behind one of the benches.

'Now, how are things with you?' the old scientist mutters, approaching the Macra on the operating table. He puts the clipboard down and examines the alien carefully through a pair of half-moon spectacles. 'Hope you're not too uncomfortable there, old thing.'

'He doesn't look at all comfortable,' says the Doctor. Somehow he has appeared at the old man's elbow, peering at the Macra alongside him.

'Who are you?'

'I'm the Doctor. Who are you?'

'Professor Greif. What are you doing in my laboratory?'

'I'm the gas man,' the Doctor replies, showing him his psychic paper. 'Routine safety inspection.'

If you want to check out the psychic paper yourself, click on box F and enter code word GAS MAN.

Or go to 140.

'No, wait,' the Doctor insists. 'We really need to check this out first. This reading could be important.'

He holds the sonic screwdriver up and the signal grows ever stronger. 'This way!'

Amy and you follow him to another door – which leads straight outside. It's good to get a bit of fresh air, but the Doctor's already off, following the screwdriver signal.

'What is it?' Amy asks as you hurry through the maze of industrial pipes and valves.

'Alien life form,' responds the Doctor.

You can hardly believe your ears. What, really?

'Some kind of proto-omnivore with a highly developed central cortex,' the Doctor gabbles. 'I think.'

He shakes the sonic screwdriver as if it might be faulty.

'Should we check that my friends are all safe?' you ask, beginning to worry.

'The school party,' Amy agrees. 'They could be in danger, Doctor.'

'This way!' the Doctor calls over his shoulder.

Follow the Doctor to 7.

You take your chance and run for it!

The sudden movement takes everyone by surprise — except the Doctor. He uses the distraction to grab Amy and together they dash through the open door with you.

Clang! You slam shut the door and the Doctor locks it with the sonic screwdriver.

You can hear angry banging on the other side but you're safe — for the moment.

'What's this?' wonders Amy. She's standing next to a long, low cabinet — not unlike a chest freezer. There are some electronic devices attached to the lid, full of blinking LEDs and controls.

'These are controls for a stasis field,' remarks the Doctor, examining the casket. 'There's something in here — and it's been kept in a state of suspended animation.'

He's already sonicing the controls to unseal the casket.

'Doctor — is that wise?'

'We have to find out what's going on here,' he insists.

The casket unlocks and opens with a hiss of cold air.

As the steam dissipates, you all peer into the casket...

Find out what's inside on 83!

'Let's go,' says the Doctor.

The three of you try to creep away, hoping the Macra won't follow. But some of the closer specimens have seen you now and decide to give chase. Their legs scrabble across the shingle, scattering pebbles with the speed of their sideways movement.

'Hurry!' says Amy.

The three of you scramble up the rocks with the Macra in pursuit. You can hear them scraping and scratching their way up behind you!

Further along the beach are some narrow caves in the cliff face. The Doctor leads you straight to them.

'We should be able to fit in here – but the Macra won't!'

'Are you sure?' Amy asks. 'It doesn't look safe!'

'Trust me!' The Doctor disappears into one of the narrow fissures. Without hesitation, you and Amy follow him – and not a moment too soon, because there's a Macra right on top of you!

It slams into the cave entrance, dislodging rocks and sand. Its claws snap desperately into the opening, searching for anything it can get a grip on.

'It's a tight squeeze!' gasps the Doctor, trying to fit through the narrowing rock.

'I can see something up ahead,' says Amy. 'Some sort of light…'

If Amy squeezes through the crack first, go to 143.

If you want to go first, try 61.

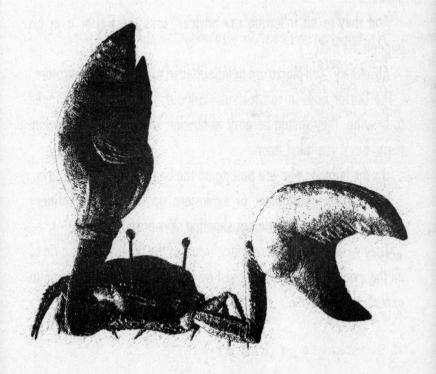

The UNIT helicopters circle the refinery, the sound of their rotor blades buzzing like angry wasps.

You, the Doctor and Amy are with Captain Stone in the lead chopper. GasTech guards are shooting at the helicopters from the ground but Stone says they don't pose a threat.

'UNIT troops have already infiltrated the deeper levels of the refinery complex,' Stone says — you can hear him through your headphones. 'They've encountered Macra, but only in isolated pockets.'

'And they're all following my advice?' asks the Doctor over his headphone mike.

'Absolutely — all Macra are being subdued with oxygen generators.'

The Doctor nods in satisfaction. 'Without the toxic gas they need to breathe, they should be easy to handle. The oxygen will weaken them, but it won't kill them.'

'It's the humans who are putting up the biggest fight,' Stone says.

As he speaks, a number of explosions rip through the refinery complex, bright orange flames shooting skywards.

'They're destroying the refinery,' realises the Doctor. 'Getting rid of all the evidence. I suppose it's just as well — I wouldn't like trying to explain this lot away.'

'We've got all this under control now,' Captain Stone says. 'Can I drop you off anywhere?'

'Somewhere near the main reception,' says the Doctor. 'That's where my TARDIS is.'

'And my school party,' you add. It's a school trip you never thought would end like this!

THE END

'Amy can look after herself,' the Doctor tells you. 'Really, she's very capable for a human. She'll catch up with us soon enough.'

He leads the way into the pipe. It's very dark in here — damp, smelly and cold.

'Some kind of gas residue,' comments the Doctor, sniffing the air. There's a smell in here like rotting fruit. 'Makes sense — if I'm right, we should find something very interesting at the end of this tunnel...'

'Why? What are you looking for?'

The Doctor's voice echoes down the tunnel, 'Trouble!'

'Trouble?'

'Yeah — so I can sort it out. Gas refinery, pollution, monsters...'

'Monsters?'

'Macra, to be precise. Giant alien crab monsters — that might sound like a joke to you, but believe me, the Macra aren't funny. They're greedy, smelly, ravenous for conquest and I think they're here.' He smiles at you in the darkness. 'But try not to worry. I'm here. It's the monsters that should be worried.'

You follow him uncertainly down the pipeline until your foot strikes something soft.

'Ouch — watch what you're stepping on, mate!' It's a girl's voice. The Doctor snaps on a torch, illuminating a pretty, red-haired girl sitting on the floor of the pipe. She's rubbing her head.

'Amy!' The Doctor is delighted. 'We've been looking for you,' he adds, not too honestly. 'What are you doing here?'

'I must have blacked out – some kind of gas, I think.' She frowns. 'I was looking for you. Found anything?'

'Only my young friend here,' the Doctor replies, introducing you. The redhead's name is Amy Pond.

'Do they know how dangerous this is likely to be?' Amy asks, eyeing you carefully.

'I think I'm about to find out,' you say.

'Stick close and do whatever the Doctor tells you,' advises Amy.

'The pipe splits here,' the Doctor calls back. 'Right and left. The smell of gas is stronger this way.'

'So which way now?' Amy wonders.

And the Doctor turns to you. 'Well? Which way do you think we should go?'

If you want to take the right-hand tunnel, go to 82.

If you would prefer to try the left-hand tunnel, go to 118.

'You're lucky to be alive,' says one of the executives. 'No one's allowed in there!'

'No wonder!' the Doctor says, suddenly waking up. 'That's a fully grown Macra from the distant future! What on Earth is it doing on... Earth?'

'They're helping us,' replies the executive. 'I'm Sebastian Quipe, the Chief Exec of GasTech. Welcome to my refinery.'

'Hold on, go back a bit,' says the Doctor. 'The Macra are helping you?'

'That's right,' says one of the scientists eagerly. 'They breathe the toxic fumes that are a side effect of the gas process we use. It's a very equitable arrangement.'

'Except for the insane monster you're keeping in there,' you say, pointing at the side chamber.

'Well, except for that, yes.'

'But we're working on that particular problem,' Quipe assures them.

'With guns?' asks the Doctor, his voice full of disgust.

'We have to be prepared,' Quipe argues. 'The future of energy provision relies on us getting this right and the Macra are fundamental to its success.'

'Allow us to demonstrate,' insists the lead scientist. He leads the Doctor away into a laboratory.

If you think Quipe could be right and the Macra can help Earth, go to 113.

If you think the Macra are dangerous and it's a stupid plan, go to 90.

'Let me see if this will help convince you,' says Professor Grief. He leads the Doctor into another room. He doesn't seem surprised when you and Amy appear alongside. The professor is more interested in showing off his experiments.

'Here are my most interesting results,' he says. He shows you a large cabinet set against the wall, covered with control panels. 'Here I have been trying to discern the most useful genetic attributes of Macra and human DNA. There are not many similarities, but both species may benefit from the advantages of the other's genome.'

The Doctor frowns. 'Human and Macra DNA? I do hope you haven't attempted to combine them, professor...'

'Attempted?' the old man chuckles. 'No — I've succeeded!'

'What?'

He operates a control on the cabinet and a panel slides open. Inside, brightly-lit like a fridge, is a compartment containing a hooded figure.

'Who's that?' asks Amy uncertainly.

'It's not a case of who,' says the Doctor grimly, 'so much as what.'

He pulls off the flimsy hood — revealing the face of a nightmare beneath. Half-human and half-Macra, the face is screwed up between two halves of shell, raw red flesh surrounding a pair of unblinking black eyes.

Amy puts a hand to her mouth in shock.

Gently, the Doctor helps the pathetic figure from the cabinet. 'He's weak – and he needs urgent treatment.' He turns on the professor, speaking quietly but with great menace: 'You're in a lot of trouble, professor.'

The professor nods sadly. 'That's why I've called the guards.'

They're already banging on the door – and there's no other way out!

If you have the stomach for more, go to 73.

The right-hand tunnel leads down in a gentle slope. It's only just wide enough to stand up in, and if you reach out on either side you can touch the sides of the tube.

'It's a pipe,' realises Amy.

'Gas refinery,' says the Doctor. 'Of course it's a pipe.'

'And is that smell gas?'

'Some kind of gas, yes.' The Doctor's voice echoed thoughtfully along the passage. 'I've smelled it before - but not on this planet.'

'Wait,' you say, holding a hand out to stop the others. 'Look!'

You point at the ground in front of you. The pipe line takes a turn downwards here — a series of metal rungs set in the side of the pipe leads down into a deep well.

'This must lead to the deeper levels of the refinery,' says the Doctor.

'Another choice, then,' realises Amy. 'This time — do we carry on, or go deeper down?'

If you want to investigate the lower levels, go down to 49.

If you want to carry on along this pipe, go to 92.

You help Amy push workbenches in front of the doors. You can see them buckling under the weight of the Macra trying to get in! A gap appears between the doors and the benches are shoved backwards. A claw snaps at the air between the gap — but the creature can't quite squeeze through.

'Doctor, this isn't going to hold them for long!' yells Amy.

The Doctor gives up on the gas controls with a gasp of annoyance. 'These things are stuck fast!'

'Sonic screwdriver?' you suggest.

'No time,' he replies, as the doors are forced open another few centimetres and the Macra's eyes push through on their stalks, searching the room for human prey.

'Let's get out of here!' Amy says.

But the scientists don't want you to leave. 'Just hold on a minute!' blurts one of them. 'You can't just come in here like this and then clear off!'

The Macra forces its way through again, pincers snapping.

'Everyone needs to abandon the refinery,' snaps the Doctor. 'Do you have a public address system of any sort?'

Crash! The Macra is almost all the way through!

If you want to get out while you still can, hurry to 43.

If you think you should alert the rest of the refinery now, go to 96.

'Go on!' urges Amy. 'Get back to the tour — we'll catch up with you later!

She's already running after the Doctor, and in a moment they've both disappeared — as if they had never been there in the first place.

'What's going on?' asks Mr Jones. 'Who was that?'

'No one,' you reply. But you know you'll see the Doctor and Amy again — and soon. But what are they up to?

'We'd better get back to the Control Tower,' says Mr Jones testily. 'We've wasted a lot of time looking for you. Come on!'

You follow them all back to the reception area, where a tall man in a grey suit is waiting. He has dark, glittering eyes and silver hair.

'My name is Sebastian Quipe,' he says. 'And this is my company. Welcome to GasTech!'

Sebastian Quipe begins his speech about GasTech — how the company has revolutionised the save conversion of oil into gas using brand new techniques devised by a team of top scientists. 'And there are absolutely no toxic side effects,' he promises. 'In fact, GasTech is the safest energy producer the world has ever known.'

Someone taps you on the shoulder. A man in a GasTech uniform puts a finger to his lips and beckons you through a side door. It's the door marked NO UNAUTHORISED ACCESS. Perhaps he's got a message from the Doctor and Amy for you...

Go and find out on 9.

Inside a vast, hi-tech laboratory, the Doctor is conferring with a number of white-coated scientists.

There are computer screens lining the walls, showing images and diagrams of the gas refinery – and the Macra!

'Don't be alarmed,' the Doctor tells you. He has to raise his voice a little to be heard over the sound of banging and clattering from the next room. 'It's quite exciting, really.'

He introduces you both to one of the scientists, Professor Banahan.

'We're using the Macra to soak up the poisonous by-products of the refinery as it converts natural liquid gas into energy,' the Professor explains. 'The Macra's special biology means that they can live here safely and help benefit the environment. It's a perfect kind of symbiosis – one can't survive without the other.'

'But what's that banging all about?' asks Amy.

'Ah, well, that's just a slight problem,' the Doctor admits. 'The Macra are a bit upset – understandable, really, with the three of us running around loose like this. The poor things just need calming down. So I think we should have a little chat with them, don't you?'

Interview with the Macra – on 84!

As Amy runs after the school party, you quickly follow the Doctor as he darts through the complicated tubes and pipes of the refinery. He keeps stopping every few yards to check the pipes with his sonic screwdriver, or to rest an ear against one to listen.

'What can you hear?' you ask.

'The end of the human race as we know it,' he replies ominously. And then he's off again, scampering through the tanks and tubes, searching, searching...

'But what are you looking for?'

'Questions! Good, like questions, keep 'em coming.'

'Some answers would be good, too.'

'Yeah,' the Doctor nods distractedly. 'I'd like answers as well. We have a lot in common, you and me.'

Suddenly you both skid to a halt as a loud scream of fear echoes through the refinery. It sounds like a child's cry – and then there's more, many more, cries and shouts and screams... and a terrible roar, as if some wild beast is loose!

'This way!' The Doctor races through the refinery, heading directly towards the commotion.

As you round the corner, you're met with a scene of devastation:

There are school kids everywhere, running wild, fearful, crying, looking for a way out.

Behind them is something impossible, awful – a giant creature, the size of a family car, covered in a thick shell, a pair of huge, snapping pincers rearing above it like the stings of a scorpion.

'Macra!' exclaims the Doctor.

Amy comes running towards you, panic on her face. 'It attacked the school party! There was nothing I could do!'

The creature – the Macra – lets out a bellowing roar, its mandibles clattering wildly, spraying noxious slime. One of its giant claws snatches up a school kid and throws him roughly aside. Then it charges forward on its six curled legs – straight for you!

'Look out!' shrieks Amy.

Go to 93.

'Don't get distracted, Doctor,' warns Amy, pointing at the hatchway.

'Don't get distracted?' the Doctor echoes peevishly. 'You drive me to distraction, you do.'

He harrumphs and then uses the sonic screwdriver to open the hatch. 'This way!' he says, leading you both into a dark, circular opening. It looks like the interior of a giant pipe. 'And that's exactly what it is,' the Doctor affirms, his voice echoing down the steel tunnel as he switches on a torch. 'One of the major refinery pipes for liquid gas, I should think.'

'Why isn't it full of liquid gas, then?' you ask.

'Good question. Let's see if we can find out!'

You move cautiously along the pipeline, the three of you contained in the small pool of light from the Doctor's torch. Everywhere else is blackness.

'Could go on for miles,' the Doctor comments airily.

Not very reassuring!

'Shh,' says Amy suddenly. 'Listen.'

A series of loud, echoing clangs reverberates down the pipe.

'That doesn't sound good,' you say.

'No way to tell which direction it's coming from either,' says Amy.

'Then, in this instance, we have no choice,' the Doctor says. 'We must carry on...'

Carry on to 118.

'Sorry,' says the Doctor. 'I can't allow that to happen. The people of this world have a right to carry on existing as they are. And besides, Earth's my favourite planet. So you lot can just clear off and be quick about it!'

The Macra clacks its mandibles angrily. 'Our research shows that Earth has already been ruined for human use – we are merely accelerating the process. It will be perfect for Macra colonisation!'

'I said no,' replies the Doctor. He points his sonic screwdriver at a control panel. 'By my reckoning, this is where you mastermind the gas exchange. The air is pretty foul in here – for humans. But if I switch over the input and output regulators by remote control...'

The sonic screwdriver whirrs and the controls begin to operate.

The Macra panics! 'No – stop! Desist! Or you will be destroyed!'

'No!' The Doctor rounds angrily on the giant alien crab. 'You stop! Stop your invasion and get off this planet now – or you'll be the ones who are destroyed. The gas exchangers have been swapped. There's pure oxygen rushing in here now – and throughout the rest of the refinery. Fine for humans – deadly for Macra!'

The Macra hisses angrily, lashing out with its claws – but it's too late. It can sense that things have gone wrong now – and the alien begins to choke and splutter as the air changes in the silo.

'You will pay for this!' it gurgles, backing towards the teleport.

'Maybe – but not today.' The Doctor points his sonic screwdriver at the teleport controls. 'Now, fix the controls so that the teleport field catches all Macra life forms!'

Hurriedly, hissing and choking, the Macra complies. The Doctor zaps the controls with the sonic screwdriver and, with a harsh *fzzzz* of crackling teleport energy, the Macra disappears.

'Back to where he came from,' declares the Doctor happily. 'Along with any others who might be hanging around too.'

With a single sweep of his sonic screwdriver, he deactivates the rest of the Macra machinery. All is now quiet.

'Amy and I can tidy up here — make sure nothing falls into the wrong hands.' He shakes your hand with a smile. 'Time for you to rejoin the tour, I'm afraid.'

But you don't mind — it's been quite interesting, for a school trip!

THE END

'Try this,' says the Doctor, rummaging in a drawer by the boat's steering wheel and coming up with a stubby-looking pistol. He tosses it to you.

'A flare pistol?' says Amy.

'Well, we are in distress,' the Doctor tells her.

The pistol is loaded with a flare. You'll only have one shot. You steady yourself against the steering wheel, gripping it with one hand as the boat jumps and bounces over the choppy sea. It's difficult to aim properly like this!

But the Macra present a big target. When the next one emerges in a flurry of salt water, you squeeze the pistol's trigger. There's a sharp crack! And the gun jolts in your hand. The flare bursts into an incandescent flower of light on the surface of the water in front of the Macra, and the creature reels back, squealing, momentarily blinded.

Sensing the weakened state of their comrade, the other Macra — every one a savage beast — converge on it. Their massive claws rip it to shreds in a boiling foam of scarlet sea water.

'That was horrible,' says Amy.

'It was necessary,' says the Doctor grimly. 'Steer us towards the beach.'

You turn the wheel, heading to the shore.

Go to 76.

At the end of this pipeline is a circular hatch with a large, central cogwheel lock. At a nod from the Doctor, you spin the wheel and the hatch creaks open on a rusted hinge.

'Welcome,' intones a deep, resonant voice from the darkness beyond. You step out of the pipe into a low chamber. There is a large, recessed tank full of water in the middle of the room. It's pretty gloomy in here but the voice continues reassuringly:

'You are quite safe. We mean you no harm.'

The Doctor shines his torch on a huge, crab-like creature squatting in the pool. It has huge, serrated claws and a pair of eyes waving on the ends of stalks.

And it chuckles as you recoil in fear.

'Do not be alarmed.'

'Are you a Macra?' the Doctor asks incredulously.

'That is correct.'

'Sorry,' the Doctor replies. 'You're remarkably friendly compared to others of your species I've met...'

'I am Kchak-naa,' replies the giant crab. 'I represent the Alliance of Intelligent Macra.'

'AIM for short?'

'No. AOIM.'

'Oh.'

'We are here to help mankind – but there may be difficulties in convincing the human race that we mean well.'

'Looking like giant crabs isn't going to help,' Amy admits.

The Doctor turns to you, raising an eyebrow. 'Well? What do you think?'

If you believe Kchak-naa's story, follow the Doctor to 123.

If you think the Macra could be lying, go to 86.

The writhing mass of infant Macra suddenly seems to sense – as one – the intrusion. The closest are crawling up the side of the cave towards you, their legs clattering across the rock.

'Doctor – look!'

You both whirl around to see Kchak-naa's eyes glowing a fierce, angry red.

'Uh-oh,' mutters the Doctor. 'Looks like it was a pack of lies after all!'

The Macra lets out a baying roar of pure hatred – casting a spray of foul-smelling saliva across the cavern.

'Run!' bellows the Doctor, and you need no second bidding. The three of you hare off across the edge of the cave, scrambling over the uneven ground, slipping and sliding, trying not to tumble into the waves of Macra snapping at your heels.

'Move!' yells the Doctor, pushing both you and Amy forward, powering you to – where?

'That crack on the rock wall – and hurry!'

Now you see it – a narrow black fissure dead ahead. The Macra are rising behind you – a flowing sea of pink, scuttling and scraping across the rocky floor. They're scrambling over each other in their haste to get to you – *and devour you alive!*

You leap into the cave entrance. It's a narrow tunnel – and it splits in two different directions!

One heads up at an angle – it looks like a very steep climb but you can feel a breath of cold, fresh air on your face.

The other tunnel heads down – easier and quicker.

Which way will you go?

Go up to 76.

Go down to 34.

You take a deep breath and step into the darkness.

'I can't see a thing,' you say.

You can hear the Doctor stepping in behind you. His voice echoes in the blackness. 'I think I've got a torch here somewhere, hang on.'

A torch light suddenly flicks on and illuminates a scene from a nightmare.

An immense crab-like creature rears above you in the darkness. The light glistens off a hard, shiny red carapace. There's a wide, sucking orifice at the front, full of sharp mandibles strung with grey drool; above it are a pair of shining black eyes on the end of wavering stalks.

But worst of all are the enormous, serrated claws raised high in the air above you, snapping like a pair of gigantic shears!

'Macra!' exclaims the Doctor, his voice full of both fear and excitement.

A girl hurries forward into the torchlight – auburn hair, short skirt, very pretty. You guess this must be Amy.

'Doctor!'

'What are you doing here?' he shouts. 'Look out!'

He grabs her as one of the Macra's giant pincers snaps overhead – but the claw hits him hard on the side of the skull and he collapses.

Amy turns, holding the Doctor's sonic screwdriver. The Macra roars angrily...

If you think Amy should try using the sonic screwdriver, go to 101.

If you think you should concentrate on the Doctor, go to 37.

'It's too far to jump,' you say, looking down at the dizzying drop. 'We'll never make it!'

Then Doctor looks back at the monster on the silo. 'Then we fight!'

The Macra is snarling angrily, swiping at you with its long arms. The heavy claws clash against the metal of the catwalk you're standing on, striking sparks.

The Doctor looks at the bright flashes for a second and then has an idea.

'Help me turn on the gas valves!' he says, darting to the end of the gantry where there is a cluster of metal rings — valves controlling the output of gas from the silo.

But you're also nearer the Macra.

'Look out!' screams Amy.

A claw whistles overhead, missing your skull by centimetres. If it had connected, you would be dead.

The Doctor's opening an access hatch on the rim of the silo with his sonic screwdriver. He signals to you with a nod and you start turning the wheel valves. There is an immediate, sharp hiss of escaping gas.

'What now?' you yell.

'Get out of here!'

The Doctor grabs you by the scruff and together you race back along the gantry towards Amy.

Behind you, the Macra lunges once again. It's incensed by your presence. But one of its massive pincers scrapes along the catwalk, drawing more sparks. The fragments of red hot metal come into contact with the gas and...

WHUMPF!

The gas ignites!

There is a roar of flame and heat. You, Amy and the Doctor duck down, covering your heads.

The Macra is engulfed by the fire. It screams, lurching backwards. It thrashes from side to side, toppling from the silo, and falls to the ground below like a huge, multi-legged comet. It lands in a blazes heap and lies still.

Carry on to 45.

You can hear a strange noise up ahead, just around the next cove.

It's a clacking, rustling sound, but it sounds wet, too, as if what's happening is taking place in the water.

The Doctor signals you to keep low, and, crouching down, you and Amy join him behind some rocks overlooking the cove.

What you see is a rock pool full of Macra – crawling all over each other, legs and arms waving blindly in the air. But there's something wrong. Some of the Macra shells appear to be loose – cracked, semi-transparent segments of shell falling away from the writhing creatures.

'What's happening?' you ask in a whisper.

The Doctor replies with a low voice: 'Amazing! What we're witnessing is quite incredible – adult Macra shedding their shells!'

'I didn't know crabs shed their shells,' said Amy.

'Some do. But the Macra aren't crabs, strictly speaking. This is the way they build and harden their shells.'

As you watch, a Macra crawls out from under its shell. Its back is white and soft, covered in thick veins, flexing slightly as the muscles of its legs move below.

'Once exposed to the air, the new shell will turn as hard as rock,' the Doctor explains softly. He's clearly fascinated, and overjoyed to witness the strange ordeal...

If you want to stay and watch, go to 98.

If you think you should move on, go to 105.

'Well,' says the Doctor, smiling. 'It's nice to see that the universe isn't all bad. Welcome to Earth.'

The Macra bows its eyes peacefully.

'Not that I can promise you a quiet time here,' the Doctor continues. 'They can be a pretty unpredictable lot, these humans. Fine one minute – all poetry, theatre, sport and peaceful scientific research... the next minute, all politics, disputes, strikes and open warfare. Just watch your step – all six of them.'

'I will take your advice,' the Macra rumbles. 'But first let me show you this...'

He leads the way back through the tank room, walking sideways with remarkable agility. Soon he has taken you to a large elevator, which he uses to descend several hundred feet below the refinery.

'Is this the guided tour?' wonders the Doctor, as you feel your ears popping. Noticing your discomfort, he smiles. 'Just swallow and it'll help equalise the pressure in your inner ear.'

'This way,' rumbles the Macra as the lift slows to a halt at the bottom of the long shaft.

'Inner 'ere?' quips the Doctor, following jauntily.

What you see takes your breath away.

It's a vast underground cavern. And it's full of tiny Macra – a vast, seething carpet of pink crabs, crawling and climbing over one another.

'Horrible!' whispers Amy.

'It's a breeding colony,' gasps the Doctor. His eyes are wide. 'There's millions of 'em!'

Leave while you still can, on 119.

The Macra are already surging through the narrow gap behind you —
in the dim light of the Doctor's torch you can see their snapping claws
and scrabbling legs, and hundreds of tiny black eyes.

'Think of something!' screams Amy.

'I'm on it!' yells the Doctor. He whips out his sonic screwdriver and
points it at the roof of the cave. 'Cover your heads and get well back!'

You do as he says — as the cave is filled with the shrill whine of the
sonic. Everything seems to shake — grit and dust falls from the roof.

'What are you doing?' you ask, covering your ears.

'Resonating the rock! If I get just the right frequency—'

Suddenly the roof of the cave falls in — weakened by the sonic
waves, chunks of rock break loose and crash down on the invading
Macra. They are crushed by the rocks and then the fissure is completely
blocked by the debris.

Coughing and choking as dust fills the air, you back away with the
Doctor and Amy.

'That's stopped the Macra all right,' says Amy. 'But where do we go
now? We're trapped!'

'I've got another idea!' says the Doctor. He makes another
adjustment to the sonic screwdriver. The tip glows green and pulses...

Find out what he's up to on 87.

'Stay where you are,' orders the Doctor. There's no arguing with that tone of voice — and there's a look of steely determination in those deep-set eyes.

The lift doors slide open. A squad of soldiers in dark combat uniforms fan out, covering the entire workshop with automatic weapons.

The leader approaches you, automatic pistol aimed at the Doctor's head. 'Rank,' he says sternly.

The Doctor raises his hands slowly. 'I don't have a rank,' he replies. 'I'm just the Doctor.'

'I mean my name is Rank,' says the soldier. 'Sergeant Kyle Rank. I'm in charge of security at the refinery.'

'GasTech's finest?'

'You could say that. You're under arrest.'

'Are you responsible for this?' asks the Doctor, indicating the Macra on the table. 'Because if you are...'

'If I am... what?' sneers Rank. He tightens his finger on the trigger.

'Don't shoot him,' you say quickly. Your mouth is as dry as dust and your heart is pounding.

The soldier laughs cruelly. 'I'm not gonna shoot him,' he says. 'The boss has got something better in mind for you lot...'

You're all led out of the workshop and through a set of security doors. You are told go through into a small, bare cell. The floor is swilling in water. It looks grim — but they've got guns and one false move could earn you a bullet...

If you think you should do as you are told, go straight to 95.

If you think you should try and make a break for it, take your chance on 63.

It's a long swim. By the time you reach the far side, you are freezing. You can't stop shivering as you climb out of the water on to a rocky bank. You're miserable and cold and wet – and so is Amy.

The Doctor looks like he's just had a refreshing dip in the hotel pool. He's soaked through and his hair is plastered to his head, but his eyes are bright and full of adventure.

'How come we can see?' stutters Amy. Her teeth are still chattering.

'Light from up ahead somewhere,' says the Doctor. He climbs a little way up the rock, his boots squelching. 'Aha! Come and see!'

Numb with the cold, you clamber up after him. The light is shining down from what looks like a steel chimney – a narrow metal shaft rising right up through the rock for hundreds of metres.

'Some kind of ventilation shaft,' says the Doctor eagerly. 'And it's got a ladder!'

Indeed, there are metal rungs set in one side of the shaft, leading right up into the distance.

'Come on!' The Doctor leads the way, scampering quickly up the narrow tube.

Wearily, still dripping, you and Amy follow.

It's a long, hard climb – your arms and legs are aching by the time you reach the top. You can barely feel your fingers – but at least you're a lot warmer!

The Doctor helps you out of the top of the pipe. You're in an antechamber for the ventilation system. There's a door leading to a passageway headed RESEARCH AREA. And there's another ventilation hatch set in the opposite wall, standing open...

If you want to investigate the research area, head for 100.

If you want to explore the ventilation system further, go to 39.

'Wait,' says the Doctor, as the door opens.

A group of men in suits – gas company executives – file in. 'Good afternoon,' says Sebastian Quipe, the company director. 'I see you found our pet Macra.'

'Rather too late, I'm afraid. It's dead,' the Doctor says flatly.

'Yes, well that one was rather a handful,' Quipe replies dismissively. 'But not to worry. There's bound to be the odd mistake.'

'That's a very callous attitude,' remarks Amy.

Quipe smiles. 'It's business, my dear. The Macra are very useful. They thrive in the poisonous fumes our refinery creates, breathing it all in. So there's absolutely no toxic waste – which can only be good for Earth, can't it? Affordable, clean energy. Isn't that what everybody wants?'

'Not at the cost of lives – any lives,' replies the Doctor, glaring darkly at the dead Macra.

'An experiment – nothing more,' Quipe says. 'The real deal is in here.' He gestures towards a grille set in the floor of the chamber. At a signal, one of the scientists accompanying the execs unlocks and opens the grille. You can hear a strange, urgent scrabbling sound from inside the hole – like a hundred legs clawing at the edges.

And then – suddenly – they come surging out of the hole in the ground! Hundreds of miniature Macra, like crabs the size of dogs, pincers snapping and legs clattering across the concrete.

Quipe laughs as you, the Doctor and Amy all start backing away, up the ramp leading to the door. The Macra scurry towards you...

Go to 57.

You follow the Doctor and Amy into a dark, low tunnel. Your footsteps echo crazily and you keep bumping your head on the metal ceiling.

You all halt at the sound of a low, bestial grow from up ahead.

'Uh-oh,' says Amy. 'I'm guessing that's not your stomach rumbling, is it, Doctor?'

'Not my stomach, no,' replies the Doctor quietly. 'Can't vouch for him though.' He shines a torch down the tunnel, and the light falls on a huge, murky red shape – hard, domed shell, spindly legs, and two enormous claws.

'Macra! In the tunnel!' Amy hisses.

'Don't panic,' the Doctor tells her. 'Don't want to frighten it, do we?'

He ventures slowly forward. The Macra shifts backwards down the pipe, claws scraping loudly on the metalwork. Another low growl reverberates down the tunnel.

'If only we had a weapon of some kind,' you say.

'I don't like weapons,' says the Doctor.

'But if it's kill or be killed...?'

If you think you should tackle the Macra, go to 31.

If you think you should try talking to it first, go to 68.

'Jump!' orders the Doctor. And without hesitating, he turns and leaps off the gantry. 'Geronimo!'

The Macra reaches out with its massive claws, snapping at the air behind him.

It's now or never. Grabbing Amy by the hand, you both leap together.

There is a moment of sickening fear as you hurtle through the air. Below, the Doctor has landed neatly on the next gantry, executing a perfect forward roll. By the time you and Amy hit the metal catwalk, he's already up and on his feet.

'Come on – this way!'

Every bone in your body feels like its vibrating with the impact. You stagger to your feet, holding on to Amy for support.

But the Macra is crawling down the side of the gantry after you! Its sharp legs grip the metal as it moves, sparks scraping. Its pincers snap and grab at you.

Run!

'In here!' yells the Doctor, throwing open a doorway in the silo at the end of the catwalk. You race towards it...

Race to 128.

The Doctor's curiosity has clearly got the better of him. He insists on checking to see what's happened.

Cautiously, you open the door to the storage tank.

Silence.

You all step carefully into the darkness once more. Gradually your eyes become accustomed to the lack of light.

The Macra is still there – but it's not moving. In fact, it's flat out – crumpled in a heap of legs and claws, like a dead crab washed up on the quayside.

'Careful, Doctor,' warns Amy as he creeps closer.

The Doctor gently examines the carcass. 'It's dead,' he says. 'How sad...'

He runs the sonic screwdriver over the body, taking readings. 'Some sort of massive cardiac arrest – it was getting pretty stressed, I suppose. But even so... tragic.'

'It was horrible,' Amy says.

'To you,' the Doctor admits. 'To another Macra, it could have been the crustaceous equivalent of Brad Pitt.'

At that moment the door on the far side of the chamber unlocks and begins to open...

The Doctor looks up. 'Could be trouble,' he whispers.

Quick – make a hasty retreat to 3.

Or you wait and see what's coming through the door on 127.

You grab hold of the giant metal wheel with the Doctor and heave. It won't budge!

'What about the sonic screwdriver?' you say.

'It's a sonic screwdriver, not a sonic torque wrench,' replies the Doctor through gritted teeth. But then his eyes widen and his eyebrows shoot up. 'Oh, but wait a second! I've just had a brilliant idea. I could use the sonic screwdriver to resonate the steel bearings that allow the wheel to move!'

And then the Doctor's already sonicing away at the mechanism.

'Hurry!' yells Amy from the far side of the room. The doors are buckling under the Macra onslaught.

'Loose!' declares the Doctor, and you heave on the wheel. With a grinding screech of metal on metal, the valve slowly turns.

The toxic gas flowing through the refinery is cut off at source.

'Now for the oxygen!' The Doctor scampers around to another valve. Luckily this one turns easily. Oxygen rushes in with a loud roar.

The Macra start to squeal, then choke and gurgle as their precious poison atmosphere rapidly disperses. The Doctor opens the double doors and one of the giant crabs collapses at his feet with a pathetic rattle.

'How the mighty are fallen,' he says quietly. And you can hear in his voice the steel of a man who does not deal with monsters lightly – alien *or* human.

It doesn't take long for the Doctor to close down the whole operation. This pale, academic-looking man seems to have taken control of the entire refinery. No one questions him – although someone will, eventually. Either the GasTech authorities or the government, or even Amy. But by then his job is done. And so is yours.

You shake hands with the Doctor and his friend by the police box in reception.

'So glad you could help,' says the Doctor, full of the enthusiasm of a man who does not go looking for trouble – but is delighted when he finds it. 'Must be going.'

Amy smiles and says goodbye. 'The Macra are no more, and the refinery is being taken over by another company. It's going to be completely rebuilt, apparently. You may get to visit it again on another school trip.'

'I hope not!' you say, as the pair of them disappears into the police box – and then it disappears too...

THE END

When you reach the reception area, the Doctor storms straight in and heads to the control centre. He is thunderously angry, and Amy and you are both swept along with him.

He throws open the double doors, scattering white-coated scientists. Executives turn to glare at him, not at all happy with the sudden intrusion. The school party, with Mr Jones the teacher, are in here too. They all turn to look at you.

The chief executive of GasTech, Sebastian Quipe, steps forward. 'Call the guards!'

'Don't bother, they've done enough damage already,' Amy warns.

The Doctor speaks quietly but firmly, with steel in his voice. 'Take me to your leader.'

'I'm afraid I don't know what you mean,' Quipe says smoothly.

But the Doctor's in no mood for a discussion. 'Think I haven't worked out what's going on here?' he demands. 'Toxic gas, genetic experiments, giant crabs...? Do me a favour!'

He marches over to a complex piece of equipment surrounded by scientists. They rush out of his way like nervous geese as he approaches. 'Advanced alien technology,' snorts the Doctor. 'I expected that, too.'

'What is it?' you ask.

'Teleport device,' says the Doctor. He's already got his sonic screwdriver out and is working at the complex control panel. The machine hums into life. 'If they won't take me to their leader,' he says, 'then perhaps their leader will come to me!'

The teleport begins to operate and a bright nimbus of light appears in the centre of the lab...

Find out what's materialising on 94.

'He's all right,' says Amy, checking the old man. 'I think he's just seasick.'

'He looks a bit green,' you agree.

The Doctor's frowning. 'So long as he's not green and spiky – that could mean he's really a Vinvocci!'

You're not really sure what the Doctor's talking about – but at least the professor seems to be recovering. He smiles weakly. 'Never was much good in boats.'

'Or in a laboratory,' counters the Doctor. 'Some of your experiments leave a lot to be desired, professor.'

'What's that up ahead?' wonders Amy, pointing.

The speedboat has travelled quite a way from the inlet. Behind you is the refinery, built on the coast. But in front of you appears to be a small island – craggy and cold-looking.

'Let's check it out,' says the Doctor, opening the throttle. The boat surges forward, kicking up icy seaspray as it veers towards the island.

You reach a shingly beach and the speedboat grounds. The Doctor switches off the engine and you all hop out.

'It looks deserted,' says Amy.

'I very much doubt it,' says Professor Greif.

Suddenly, figures emerge from the sand dunes and from behind the reeds on the headland. Dark uniforms and red berets – and all carrying hi-tech weaponry.

'Unified Intelligence Taskforce!' the Doctor cries. 'UNIT! What are you lot doing here?'

'I had them on standby all the time,' the old man smiles. 'I'm a UNIT scientific advisor, working undercover at GasTech.'

'Excellent,' replies the Doctor. 'UNIT's just what we need. Let's get back across to the mainland and get the party started!'

If you trust the professor's claims, go to 27.

If you think he's bluffing, go to 71.

'I've been doing my best with very limited resources,' says the professor. His shoulders slump dejectedly.

'Surely GasTech can supply you with anything,' argues Amy. 'They're a big company – they must have oodles of cash.'

'GasTech is nearly in administration,' the old man sighs. 'If I don't find a solution to the toxic gas crisis, then the refinery will close down, hundreds of people will lose their jobs – and the Macra will all starve.'

But while the professor's talking, you've noticed that the Macra on the examination table is beginning to wake up! Its legs are clutching uselessly at the air and its claws begin to click.

The Doctor's seen it too. 'Look out, professor – your Macra chum is coming to...'

It happens incredibly quickly – one minute you're pointing towards the Macra, and the next thing it's lashing out with one of its long, armoured claws. The ties that bind it snap as the creature rolls free.

'It's loose!' cries the professor, horrified. And with a thud! one lashing claw strikes him on the head. The old man crashes to the floor, stunned.

The Macra roars, smashing from side to side to free itself from the last of its bonds.

If you want to help the professor, go to 6.

If you think you should leave him and get out quick, go to 55.

You hit the floor with a blinding pain in your head.

You try to get up but your vision is blurred. A huge armoured shape moves in front of you, and there is a horrible, gurgling roar.

Desperately you try to crawl away – anywhere, somewhere…

But then you feel the cold, hard grip on your ankle, and you are dragged back towards the monstrous form. Your fingers try to dig into the floor, but the strength of the thing is irresistible.

You turn to face the terrible shape, knowing the end must be near…

And then you black out completely.

Go to 97.

You set to work, discovering the access code very quickly. But while the Doctor is watching you work, something stirs behind you...

'Look out!' cries Amy.

The Macra lurches back to life with an ugly snarl, its pincers clacking. Its legs scrabble for a grip but it's unsteady – clearly still feeling the effects of the oxygen. It smashes several trays of instruments and a computer across the room in its spasm.

The Doctor points his sonic screwdriver at the beast – and a shrill whine fills the air. The tip pulses bright green and the Macra subsides once more...

'Just needed a little extra persuasion,' smiles the Doctor. 'Now let's get back to work...'

Go to 16.

You step through the doors and your breath is taken away — it's impossible! The room you are in is simply huge; much bigger than the outside. At the centre is a complicated hexagonal control console with a central glass column. There is complex instrumentation arranged all over the console.

The Doctor's already busy at the controls. 'Just a short hop — shouldn't be too difficult!'

'It does take a bit of getting used to, doesn't it?' Amy asks.

You nod mutely.

The Doctor checks a scanner screen, showing a detailed map of the refinery. 'Where do you think would be best? Central laboratory section — or underground?'

If you want the TARDIS to materialise in the laboratory complex, go to 11.

If you want to land underground, go to 88.

'We'll have to be careful from here,' the Doctor says as you near the complex. 'There will probably be guards...'

You crouch down as you run, hurrying across to the nearest building. The refinery looks like a huge tangle of metal pipes and silos. Smoke pours from a number of steel chimneys towering overhead.

'There's a fire escape door here,' Amy realises.

Go to 3.

The man in the tweed jacket and bow tie is hurrying towards a doorway at the back of the room.

No one else is watching him except you.

The man takes some kind of instrument out of a pocket and uses it to unlock the door. You hear a sharp whine and see a green glow coming from the tip of the pen-like device. Then he's gone.

This is all much more interesting than Sebastian Quipe's speech.

So what are you going to do?

If you want to take a closer look at the Police Box, go to 42.

If you want to follow the man in the tweed jacket, go to 17.

Professor Greif squints carefully at the psychic paper - but the Doctor's already talking: 'Must be a pain trying to deal with those claws. Bet they can give you a nasty nip if you're not careful!'

'The Macra is perfectly safe under these conditions,' Greif argues. He's still not sure about that ID card, but he can't help talking about his experiments. 'It is secured for its own safety. We are trying to understand the ways in which they can benefit mankind by absorbing the toxic fumes the refinery produces. Do you not approve?'

The Doctor pulls a face. 'Let's just say I'm not convinced.'

If Professor Greif as good as he seems? If you're not convinced, check out 109.

If you want to hear more about the professor's work, try 134.

Amy runs down on to the sand with you, chasing the Doctor. Moments later you are all splashing through the surf — but then the moment turns sour.

With a huge roar, something surges out of the water. It looks like a giant crab — six legs and two huge claws. It crashes through the waves, sending sea water showering over you.

'Get away from the water's edge!' commands the Doctor, dragging you away.

The creature splashes along the beach and then sinks back beneath the waves with a gurgling roar. Its eyes stare at you from stalks for one long, terrifying moment before disappearing into the sea.

'What was it?' asks Amy, shaken.

'A Macra,' the Doctor replies. 'Not something I ever expected to see here. Nasty alien crustaceans, up to no good! Still, perhaps it explains a fair bit… Come on!'

Follow him to 76.

Suddenly there's a loud explosion; rock and shrapnel flying everywhere. Half-choked already, you crawl away from a pall of smoke filling the cave. Dark figures move purposefully through the grey mist – they're wearing military-style respirators and carrying machine guns.

There's a harsh rattle of gunfire and shrieks from the Macra.

You feel yourself hauled to your feet by a pair of soldiers and dragged towards the exit. You're too weak to notice anything else – except the fact that the Doctor and Amy are also being bundled away. It's a rescue mission!

The soldiers drag the three of you to safety, where the leader rips off his respirator and introduces himself.

'Captain Stone – from UNIT. Pleased to meet you.'

'The Unified Intelligence Taskforce!' cries the Doctor delightedly. He shakes the captain warmly by the hand. 'Just what we need!'

A UNIT helicopter is clattering in to land. Captain Stone leads you all towards it at a run. 'We were hoping we'd find you here, Doctor,' he shouts above the noise of the rotors.

'I used to be UNIT's scientific advisor, a long time ago,' the Doctor explains to you and Amy. 'Now let's see if we can sort this lot out once and for all!'

Go with UNIT to 106.

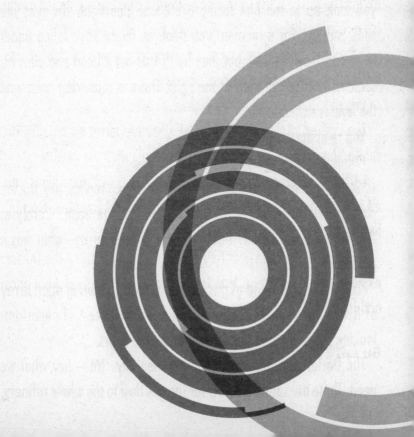

Amy squeezes through the gap, with you and the Doctor eager to follow. The light ahead is strange — mesmerising, dazzling, almost hypnotic.

'Don't look into the light!' yells the Doctor.

But you can't help it. It's calling you forward, flickering, coruscating...

Amy, too, is caught in the grip of the light.

The Doctor grabs you both and throws you to the ground. Stunned, you look up to see him facing a brilliant blue light. His eyes are wide, staring. For a moment you think he might have fallen under its strange spell as well, but then he thrusts out a hand and aims his sonic screwdriver straight at the light. There is a piercing noise and the light is extinguished.

You're in darkness.

'What was that?' gasps Amy.

'Some sort of automatic guard mechanism,' replies the Doctor, picking over the fused wires where the light had been. 'Paralyses the human brain. Luckily I'm not human. Question is — what was it guarding?'

'Looks like some kind of gas valves,' you say, pointing at an array of heavy metal wheels. They are connected to a nest of important-looking pipes. Beyond that is a set of double doors.

The Doctor rubs his hands together gleefully. 'Ha — just what we need. These are safety controls for the gas flow to the whole refinery,

I'm sure of it.'

'Whatever you're going to do, Doctor, do it quickly,' urges Amy. 'Something's trying to get through those doors — and I think it's the Macra!'

Hurry to 131.

DOCTOR ⊞ WHO

Also Available:

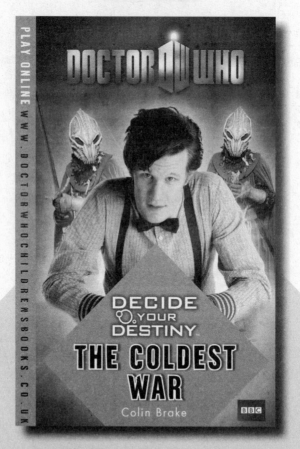

ISBN: 978-1-40590-686-9